DETE

MW01675223

Join to

for a missing teenage boy in the mad megalomaniacal East Village. As the case runs its course, the handsome Max's selfish, self-contained, self-everything life is dramatically and permanently altered through his contacts with the fantastic individuals who cross his path as they form a chain to the solution.

Not the least of these is the one, the only, the unique and magnificent Sylvia Plotkin, a high school teacher who would bring a cold sweat to Bel Kaufman's brow. When Sylvia joins Max in the hunt for the missing Tippy, mystery, murder, and mayhem are happily tempered with belly laughs.

By George Baxt

THE ALFRED HITCHCOCK MURDER CASE**

THE DOROTHY PARKER MURDER CASE*

PROCESS OF ELIMINATION

THE NEON GRAVEYARD

BURNING SAPHO

THE AFFAIR AT ROYALTIES

"I!" SAID THE DEMON**

TOPSY AND EVIL**

A PARADE OF COCKEYED CREATURES*

SWING LOW, SWEET HARRIET**

A QUEER KIND OF DEATH*

***Forthcoming from IPL Library of Crime Classics®.*
**Available in a Crime Classics® edition.*

GEORGE BAXT

A PARADE OF COCKEYED CREATURES

OR

DID SOMEONE MURDER OUR WANDERING BOY?

A CRIME CLASSIC®

INTERNATIONAL POLYGONICS, LTD.
NEW YORK CITY

A PARADE OF COCKEYED CREATURES
OR DID SOMEONE MURDER OUR WANDERING BOY?

Library of Congress Card Catalog No. 86-81921
ISBN 0-930330-47-1

Printed and manufactured in the United States of America
by Guinn Printing.
First IPL printing December 1986.
10 9 8 7 6 5 4 3 2 1

For JAY SANFORD

who thinks I'm Rona Jaffe

CHAPTER ONE

Marcus Blaney shifted from one foot to the other, nervously rubbing his sweaty palms together like an apartment-house doorman the day before Christmas. His wife sat stiffly in the straight-back chair, hands tightly clenched at either end of her alligator purse, staring at the detective behind his desk, hunched over the yellow pad, studying the notes he had accumulated during the past twenty minutes. The black armband on his jacket sleeve—Wilma Blaney wondered, who is he mourning?

Blaney ran the tip of his tongue across his lower lip, then crossed to the chair next to Wilma's and sat. Their eyes met briefly as the detective raised his slightly, watching Blaney dry his palms with a handkerchief.

Irish linen. Mattie loved Irish linen. The sheets, the pillow slips, his handkerchiefs and the boy's, Irish linen.

At the sound of cellophane ripping, the detective's eyes shifted to Blaney's nervous fingers. So we have something in common, the detective thought, a preference for the same brand of cigarettes, and that's more than most people.

Blaney held the pack toward the detective, who studied the package for a moment and then helped himself to a cigarette. Blaney fumbled in a pocket of his expensive tweed jacket for matches, but the detective was already applying the flame of his desk lighter to the cigarette tip. Wilma moved forward in her seat. When she spoke, the strained edge to her voice reminded the detective of Mattie when she was working up to an argument.

"Mr. Larsen . . ." she began.

"*Van* Larsen," Max corrected her.

She burst into tears. Blaney left his chair and knelt beside his wife, one arm around her shoulder, patting her gently just above the left breast.

(I *knew* I was right, thought Max with satisfaction. All women *are* alike. I never knew from one word to the next which would set Mattie off. Russian roulette, that's what it was like. Russian roulette. Five empty chambers go click-click-click-click-click, then *bang,* and an invisible wound drawing invisible blood and then the tears. How I hate tears. *Christ,* how I hate tears.)

He felt the pencil snap between his fingers.

Wilma Blaney stared at the two pieces of pencil where they had dropped on the pad. (He doesn't like me. He's been so rude, so matter-of-fact about Tippy's disappearance. Why doesn't he like me? Does he object to pretty women in their early forties who look ten years younger—well, that's what everybody tells me, including my mirror? Haven't I answered every one of his questions, including the damned impertinent ones—what's my date of birth got to do with Tippy's disappearance?—clearly and intelligently? Can I help it if I manage to be charming even under stress?)

"Is something wrong?" she blurted out, punctuated

by a telling sniff as she raised a lightly perfumed handkerchief to her nose.

Max nodded, tapping the pad with a fresh pencil from the Toby jug on his desk that held over thirty. "Why'd you wait five days before reporting your son missing?"

"Ask *him*," snapped Wilma, angrily indicating her husband as she popped the handkerchief back into her purse, snapped it shut and crossed her legs.

"Mr. Blaney?"

Blaney was back in the chair and squirming, his face flushing.

(Poor slob, thought Max, I'll bet there are footprints all over your back where your wife takes her daily stroll.)

"It's not the first time he's disappeared on us," croaked Blaney.

(And you look like a frog. How often has your wife kissed you, hoping you'd turn into a prince.)

Wilma spoke. "A night or two . . . that was all . . . just a night or two . . . and then he'd phone to tell us where he was or where he'd been." The tears had left Wilma's eyes and settled in her voice. "I'm sure you understand, Detective Lar . . . *Van* Larsen," grinding down on the *Van* like the heel of her shoe on a cigarette butt, "one must allow a boy of seventeen a *certain* amount of freedom."

"And if you don't allow it," Blaney added, his voice passive, "they take it anyway. He isn't exactly a wild kid . . ." (That voice. Definitely a frog. Would he be content to squat in a puddle or on a lily pad?) ". . . but most of the time he does what he damn well pleases. Leastways, he never answers to anybody about anything. Not to me, anyway."

"You never take an interest!" shouted Wilma.

"You never take an interest, Max!" he could hear Mattie shouting.

"I'm as much of a father to him as any man could be under the circumstances!" croaked Blaney, and Max sympathized. Like furious tennis players, they continued swatting back and forth their merits and demerits as parents.

"People . . . people . . ." cautioned Max, briskly tapping the pencil for order, "bickering won't help us find your son." (Like two cats on a backyard fence or playing King of the Mountain with a garbage pail. Was that how Mattie and me looked to the boy?)

Max focused on Wilma. "Would you like some coffee?"

"No, thank you." Slightly petulant, the sign of the spoiled and the overindulged.

"Coffee, Mr. Blaney?" with a note of sympathy and understanding.

Blaney shook his head and took a deep drag on the cigarette.

Max cleared his throat and studied his notes. "I'd like to go over this again to make sure I've got the facts straight. Don't hesitate to stop me if some of this needs correcting or amending."

Wilma nodded and Blaney rubbed his chin thoughtfully.

"Henry Thorpe Blaney," began Max (what a bore this is, what a damn bore), "age seventeen, height five foot eleven, weight around one hundred and sixty, eyes brown-green, hair reddish brown, complexion fair, crescent scar under left side of chin, mastoid scar behind right ear, senior at Robert Wagner High School, last seen by parents Friday, May thirteenth, wearing brown slacks, red sport shirt, blue blazer, white sneakers, white socks, carrying schoolbooks. Left home approximately eight A.M., presumably to attend school."

(Max Van Larsen, mused Wilma, studying him like a smear under a microscope. Age around forty, height around six feet or thereabouts, weight . . . weight . . . well, easily one hundred and eighty, give or take a pound or a few ounces . . . hair kind of dark blond and meticulously combed, nothing like this chubby semibald creature seated on my right . . . eyes heavenly blue but as cold as agates . . . complexion swarthy . . . manner bored and surly . . . wears a narrow wedding band . . . lucky bitch, whoever she is . . . I'd like to gallop this one around a mattress for a couple of hours . . .)

"Mrs. Blaney." His voice was politely insistent.

"Yes? Yes? What?" The words tripped over each other in the rush.

(Now what the hell's she blushing for? Max wondered).

"I asked," said Max patiently, "if you and your husband often went away on weekends without the boy."

"We went out to East Hampton to open our summer house . . ."

"I asked if you often went away on weekends without the boy."

"A few times." Petulant again. "He's always been quite capable of looking after himself." She sought corroboration in her husband's face but he was lighting a fresh cigarette. She turned back to Max. "Tippy's very mature for his age. And very independent. I . . . we . . . I encourage that in him. It's not healthy for a boy to be attached to his mother . . . his parents . . . don't you agree?"

"Let the boy alone, Mattie! Let him stand on his own two feet! For crying out loud, he'll be fourteen! It's time . . ."

"That's the way we were brought up," he heard Wilma saying, "and if I must say so myself, teaching a child to be independent is the first step on the road to maturity."

(Thank *you,* Dr. Joyce Brothers).

"There's such a thing as *too much* independence," the frog croaked. There was enough fire in Wilma's eyes to destroy Chicago again. "You should have seen what his room looked like when we got back," pursued Blaney, ignoring the arson in his wife's eyes. "It was like a hurricane hit it. Drawers were pulled out and overturned, the bed was stripped, the carpet pulled back, all the junk he kept in his closet flung all over the place."

"Like it was ransacked," contributed Max.

"He was never very tidy." Wilma knew how to jockey into position.

Max sat back, his eyes encompassing the Blaneys. "You come home Sunday evening after a two-day absence, no sign of your son, his room a shambles, and then wait until *today* before reporting his disappearance?"

"Well . . . you see . . . it's like I said," fumbled the frog. "We know Tippy . . . I mean . . . we're used to his behavior. He's torn the room apart before . . . you see . . . he's an *impatient* sort of boy. He's got this rotten temper . . . we figured he was trying to find something and when it didn't turn up . . . he got mad . . ."

"Or maybe this time somebody else went mad," suggested Max.

"Good God," gasped Wilma, "you're not thinking he might have been kidnaped!"

"Who knows," sighed Max, "it's becoming popular again. Any strange phone calls the past three days, like nobody at the other end when you answer it, anything like that?"

"Nothing," said Wilma. "There's been nothing like that at all. Of course, some of his friends have called . . . and one of his teachers . . ."

"Why did you wait three days?" persisted Max.

Wilma stared at the frog, who blinked his eyes and ran his finger around his collar as he spoke. "Because I thought I saw him yesterday."

Max leaned forward. "Where?"

"Washington Square. In the park . . . near the fountain."

"When?"

"Around noon. I . . . I was out looking for him. There was this protest rally . . . support Dr. Timothy Leary . . . somebody like that. I thought I saw Tippy with some friends at the edge of the crowd. I yelled his name . . . it was so noisy . . . so I tried elbowing my way through to him. When I got to where I thought I saw him, he was gone."

"That still leaves two days unaccounted for."

"Oh hell," muttered Blaney, "the kid's been in trouble before." Wilma was examining her fingernails. "Twice

. . . petty theft. The last time was about a year ago. I was afraid he might have been up to something again. You see, Friday morning, before we left for the Hamptons, he asked me for five hundred dollars." Max's expression remained a blank. It disturbed Blaney. "You didn't bat an eyelash."

"I don't carry a bat," said Max. "What did he want with five hundred dollars?"

"He wouldn't say!" Hands outstretched to dramatize the bewilderment. "He just acted like he had every right to expect the money! Of course I told him he'd get no such thing, and we argued and then he stormed out of the house. Wilma was up in our bedroom packing, and when I told her, she thought he must have been kidding or something."

"Well, I did," said the wide-eyed Wilma, lids straining under the weight of false eyelashes. "You see . . . his father gives him a terribly generous allowance." She brushed lint from her skirt. "Fifty dollars a week."

(Now, thought Max, I could use a bat.)

"Fifty dollars a week," repeated Max softly, "that's about a third of my weekly salary." He scratched a knee to suppress a shudder. "You think he may be staying away out of pique?"

"That's right," said Blaney, nodding. "That's what I been thinking all along, and pretty soon he'd get over it and come home. But Wilma here, she insisted we come to Missing Persons."

"*I* think he's in some kind of trouble," said Wilma, the voice strained again, "and *afraid* to come home. We have to find him and help him. We were warned if he was arrested again, no amount of influence would help him this time."

"Five hundred dollars." Max was staring at the ceiling. "Now what would a seventeen-year-old boy want with five hundred dollars?" He threw the pencil on the desk and turned to Blaney. "Tell me about the petty thefts. What did he steal and from whom?"

Frog-green turned beet-red.

"Well, tell him, darling," prodded Wilma.

Blaney cleared his throat. "He stole from me."

(If he's waiting for that to sink in, thought Max, it has sunk.)

"He'd been stealing from me all along," said Blaney. "I'm an auction dealer. You must have passed my warehouse over on West Broadway lots of times."

Max nodded.

"Tippy was free to come and go as he pleased. He used to come to the auctions and bring his friends. You know, for a lot of people, auctions give them a big charge. Fine paintings, sculpture, rugs, glassware . . ."

". . . And figurines," added Wilma. "Tippy has a taste for figurines."

Blaney's eyes darted to Wilma, then back to Van Larsen. "The first couple of times he lifted some, I got them back before he could sell them. But then," licking his lower lip again, "then he took one worth over five hundred dollars and sold it for fifty. He wouldn't tell me to who and I had to get it back. So," staring briefly at Wilma who was inspecting the tip of a shoe, "so to teach him a lesson, I called in the cops . . . the police. They . . . they were very cooperative . . ."

(Stop licking my backside, thought Max.)

". . . They knew I was really trying to help the boy—set him straight, you know. They let him off in my custody. But then the *second* time, he takes this Dresden figure worth *thousands* . . ."

"He *never* knew what the damn things were worth," snapped Wilma.

"He knew they were worth *something!*" The handkerchief was back in his hands and rubbing. "And he wouldn't tell me what he did with it. Well, what could I *do?*" Now he dabbed at his brow.

"You think he's stolen something again?"

"No," said Marcus, "he's not permitted in the warehouse or the auction rooms any more. The guards have strict orders. Anyway, even if he'd found some way to get in, if something was missing, it would have been reported by now. This time . . . this time it must be something else."

One must allow a boy of seventeen a certain amount of freedom.

"What about his friends?" asked Max. "Have you inquired around? Like did any of them see him over the weekend?"

"We don't know very much about his friends," said Wilma.

(You don't know very much about your son either, Max decided.)

"What do you know about your son? You don't give a damn about him!" Mattie standing over him in the kitchen, batter dripping from the ladle she was waving like a cutlass, small doughy puddles forming on the linoleum and the table. "Have you ever asked him if he wants to go

to one of your damned concerts, one of your damned art exhibitions, one of your damned foreign movies? What the hell makes you think you're better than everybody else? Why don't you ask him what he likes? Just once . . . ask him!" The boy sitting there, staring at the tier of lukewarm pancakes, too thin, too pale, too embarrassed.

Max shifted in his chair. "You said some of his friends called inquiring about Tippy. Didn't you ask any of them when they'd last seen him?"

"No. No, I didn't. I . . . I just said he hadn't been home . . . not for days . . ." Wilma was fumbling. "That we were worried, and if they heard from him, he was to come home right away."

"You said one of his teachers called."

Wilma nodded. "Mrs. Plotkin. He hasn't been to school since Thursday."

"Since Thursday."

"He's cut school before," interjected Blaney.

"Has she ever called before?" asked Max.

"No," said Wilma.

(But this time, thought Max, Mrs. Plotkin is curious.)

"Which of his friends do you know about?" Max directed the question at Wilma. He wondered if the frog was too stupid to notice his wife was flirting, or too nervous to give a damn.

Wilma moistened her carmine lips as she furrowed her brows in thought. "We-e-ell," she said, drawing the word out like a strand of chewing gum, "I know there's this girl he's been seeing a lot of. She works nights at some coffee house on Bleecker Street I think . . . waitress or something I guess."

"Her name?"

"Now let me think. Bibi . . ." tapping her cheek with an index finger. "Yes, it must be Bibi . . . that was the title of one of his poems."

(*Poems!*)

". . . Bibi Something."

"Your son writes poetry?"

"He's had several published in *Sappho,*" Wilma said with a trace of pride, "one of those teensy Village publications that don't pay but mean well."

"And the coffee house?"

"What about it?"

"Do you know the name?"

"Oh. Not offhand, I'm afraid. But I *think* it's in the poem. There are copies of *Sappho* somewhere in the house."

"Who else besides Bibi Something?"

Blaney leaned forward. "Lois Corey."

Max didn't miss the change of expression on Wilma's face. "Who's Lois Corey?" he asked Blaney.

"An old friend of ours," Wilma sliced in swiftly. "She's Tippy's godmother. She's a dressmaker. Tippy always runs errands for her. Things like that."

Max kept his eyes on the pad as he made notes in the scrawl only he could decipher. "Address?"

"Something Bank Street."

Max looked up. "Do you suppose there's a poem with Lois Corey's address?"

"I'm not very good at addresses or phone numbers," Wilma said, pouting, "and besides, I don't want to involve Lois in this . . . not just yet."

"Why not?"

"She's not well. She's terribly high-strung. And she has a heart condition. She's very devoted to Tippy and all this might upset her."

"You want the boy found?"

(Want a piece of candy, Wilma thought irritatedly, he just might as well be asking that. Want a piece of candy.)

"Why the hell do you think we're here?" she exploded.

Max's expression remained unchanged. "I need your full cooperation, Mrs. Blaney."

She remembered Lois Corey's address. She remembered the Cloven Hoof was the name of the coffee house on Bleecker Street. She remembered Mrs. Plotkin's first name was Sylvia. She remembered a Madame Vilna who used to be a star of the Yiddish Theater in the heyday of Second Avenue. Madame Vilna now gave dramatic readings, occasionally including Tippy's poems, and sometimes Tippy read with her. (Max kept his eyebrows from arching at this.) Wilma remembered a sculptor named Clifton Southford who once used Tippy as a model. And then she sat back with legs crossed again, skirt an inch higher, an expression on her face that seemed to beg a pat on the head or some more delectable part of her anatomy.

Max's eyes were still riveted to the pad. "No friends at school?"

"Let me think." She moistened her lips again and stared at the ceiling.

"What about the Creep?" croaked Blaney. Wilma and Max looked at him. "The one who collects obituaries."

"Oh, *him,*" snorted Wilma.

"What's his name?" asked Max.

"Ashley," said Wilma.

"First name?"

"That's his first name."

"What follows Ashley?"

"I'm thinking." Irritated again. Then she snapped her fingers. "Tybor. Ashley Tybor. And I *don't* know where *he* lives, or"—she couldn't resist adding—"if it's in a poem. Maybe Mrs. Plotkin can help you. I think he's one of her students too."

Max studied the names on the pad.

Bibi Something who works in a coffee house.

A seamstress-godmother, high-strung, with a heart condition.

A sculptor.

A teen-age necrophile.

Variety was apparently the spice of Tippy's life.

"This'll do for a start."

"Don't you want to examine Tippy's room?" asked Wilma.

"In time," said Max.

"What happens now?" asked Blaney, stubbing out a cigarette in the ashtray. (And thinking, Damned good ceramic, this cop has taste.)

"I go out looking for your son."

Wilma oozed concern. "Of course you'll keep in touch with me."

"I'll be in touch with both of you."

They left, and Max opened the window to clear the small office of cigarette smoke and expensive perfume. He opened the top drawer of the desk, found a bottle of stomach mints and popped two tablets into his mouth. Ten minutes later he completed typing in triplicate the full report of his interview with the Blaneys. Then he phoned downstairs for a copy of the record on Henry Thorpe Blaney. He checked the phone book for missing addresses to match the names supplied him by Wilma Blaney. His wristwatch told him it was not yet noon.

He decided to begin with Sylvia Plotkin. He let the desk know he'd be out most of the day, then rose and crossed to the small mirror hanging next to the Degas print. He examined himself in the mirror and was satisfied that everything was neatly in place.

Especially the black armband.

CHAPTER TWO

"And figurines," sneered Blaney, mimicking Wilma cruelly, "Tippy has a taste for figurines!"

Wilma's hands tightened on the wheel of the car as she piloted it across Eighth Street toward West Broadway. There was enough venom in her voice to kill. "Van Larsen would have found it in Tippy's record anyway. That's no dumb cop we're dealing with. We shouldn't have waited this long to report Tippy missing. We should have done it on Tuesday like I wanted to."

"Crap."

"What a fine set of parents Van Larsen must think we are."

"Up him." He flung a cigarette butt out the window. "Stinking little brat," he said, then stared through the windshield in silence.

"What do we do about Lois?"

"Up her."

Wilma bore down on the horn and then swerved to avoid hitting a cat. "I better get to her before he does. Prepare her for him. She's plenty suspicious as it is. Tippy was supposed to have lunched with her and Basil . . ."

"Basil," snorted Blaney.

". . . On Sunday and here it is Thursday. I *like* Basil. Wish to hell he'd marry Lois and put us all out of our misery."

"Up Basil."

"Up *you*," swerving to avoid hitting a pushcart peddler. "I wish I'd given Van Larsen a better snapshot of Tippy. Maybe we should run it in the *News* or something with a description."

"Maybe we'll just wait and see what your boy friend comes up with."

Wilma's eyes narrowed as she swung into West Broadway. "What do you mean 'boy friend'?"

"I ain't blind."

"You're sick."

"I ought to belt you one."

"Go ahead. I'll smash into something."

"Wish to God the little bastard had never been born."

Wilma pulled up in front of the warehouse and turned to Blaney. "Next time we see Van Larsen, we should act more concerned. I almost bust a gut forcing out the tears back in his office."

"I consoled you, didn't I?" He shoved the door open.

"You better come home for dinner."

Halfway out of the car he turned and glared at her. "You giving me orders?"

"Supposing Van Larsen decides to drop by? How'd it look if you're not home?"

"Promising."

"Pig." He was out of the car. "We're supposed to be distraught! Our son's missing!"

Blaney slammed the door shut and walked away.

(The next time, thought Wilma as she bore down on the gas, the next time I marry for love.)

When Antonia Burgess first came to work for Marcus Blaney three years before, she was fresh out of secretarial school. Marcus had compared her looks to the first blossoms on a lilac bush, one of the rare times he had ever rhapsodized. Her lush Latin face inspired comparison to an early Roman sculpture (not by Marcus, but by one of his more esthetic customers). When she crossed the thick Byzantine rug from the door to his desk, he had to hold tight to the arms of his swivel chair to keep from swooning. And when she spoke, visions of Nesselrode pie swam before his eyes.

That was three years ago.

Staring at her behind the typewriter as he entered his reception room, he wondered at the identity of the malady ravaging her face and body. Not that the metamorphosis was all that devastating. Anyone meeting her for the first time would still find her attractive, but the blossoms were beginning to tremble and flutter to the ground.

Where once a light daub of lipstick, a trace of eye shadow and a few pats of a powder puff had sufficed, there was now a heavily applied base on the face, an overexaggerated orange mouth, and four lines of mascara grotesquely emphasizing two dull and lifeless eyes. And her body. Still not bad, but then, no longer the magnet that once made heads jerk to admiring attention. Her clothes no longer seemed to take pride in being worn by her.

"'Morning," growled Marcus, slamming the door shut, "any messages?"

"They're on your desk."

Visions of cold fettucini swam before Marcus' eyes. "You sick or something?"

Her hands dropped to her lap. Had he seen them trembling? Had he heard the keyboard rattling? Were the beads of perspiration on her forehead back?

"I'm fine," she managed to say, though the voice didn't sound like her own.

"You ain't been looking so good lately," he persisted.

"I think I had a touch of virus," she stammered. (Damn me! I've got to get through this day! I've got to!)

"Then why didn't you stay home?"

"There's too much to do."

"Stop being such a martyr and take care of yourself." He hoped she wasn't working herself up to another advance in salary. She was already three weeks in hock to him.

Under the desk her fingers were now tightly interlaced. "Any news about Tippy?"

"Nothing." He entered his office and the slamming door rattled the windows and Antonia. Her fingers flew to her temples and she bit her lower lip, smearing her teeth with orange.

She didn't hear the other door opening quietly and the young man entering. He wore a brown tweed suit with frayed cuffs, and had frayed red hair that grew to just below the nape of his neck. His handsome face was marred by deep shadows under the eyes.

"Is he free?"

Antonia gasped a startled "Oh!"

He closed the door just as quietly as he had opened it. "You should have stayed home today."

"And do *what!*" she cried.

He raised an index finger to his lips, and when he spoke, she had to strain to hear him. "You look like hell, that's why you should have stayed home today."

"I'm *in* hell," she whispered frantically.

"Can you last out the day?"

She thought she detected some concern in his voice, and when she replied, her own voice held a degree of control. "I'll last."

He reached over, rubbed her shoulder gently, winked, then crossed to the door to Blaney's office and knocked. Blaney growled a muffled reply, and with another reassuring wink at Antonia, he opened the door and went in.

"I'll last," Antonia whispered to herself. "I'll last, so help me God I'll last."

Van Larsen entered the recently constructed edifice which looked like a cross between the Whitney Museum and a dentist's ranch-style residence in Mineola. The hall didn't smell the way he thought he remembered all high school hallways smelled. His had smelled dank, rancid, but somehow friendly. He had liked school. It was one of the few things he had liked as a child. Then he stared at the walls and knew this was a high school the way a high school should be. The graffiti was as profuse as it had been in his day, if more pruriently advanced.

"Can I help you?" The voice cut through him like a bow drawn across a badly tuned viola.

Van Larsen stared at the rat-faced boy with the horn-rimmed glasses, the inch-thick lenses, the mottled skin, the unkempt hair, the badge on his filthy sweater lettered "Monitor," the finger descending from his nose.

"I'm looking for Mrs. Plotkin."

"She's in class." He drew in on his nose, then coughed, and Van Larsen averted his face.

"I want to see her."

"Are you a parent?"

Max hesitated a moment before answering. "I'm a detective."

The boy pointed the still-moist finger. "Straight down that hall, room fourteen B, the next to the last door on your left. Who's in trouble?"

"You, sonny," said Max, "if you don't learn to use a handkerchief."

Sylvia Plotkin faced the enemy with the strength, the courage, the valor of an old campaigner. "Rodriguez." She spoke the name ominously, emphasizing the threat in her voice by slowly tapping a heavy ruler on her desk. "You throw one more blackboard eraser at Melvin Shimkin, and I start deportation proceedings in the morning."

Rodriguez continued leaning placidly against the blackboard, where under no circumstances or in Mrs. Plotkin's lifetime would he make X plus Y minus Z square plus double W equal the square root of F.

"And, Shimkin," declared Mrs. Plotkin, sternly fixing her eyes on the red-headed boy wearing a Batman sweater in the last seat of the last row to her right, "how many times have I told you never to use that word *spic*."

Shimkin shrugged as he spoke, wiping chalk dust from Batman's face. "He called me a *kike*."

"Children," said Sylvia Plotkin, already too late to amend that to ladies and gentlemen, "we are all in the same boat. We are Americans. And good Americans don't call each other *spic* or *kike* or *dago* or *nigger*, and how many times do I have to remind you of that? Lolita Jurado, will you stop fidgeting, you're making the whole room shake."

"There's somebody to see you," said Lolita, pointing at Max Van Larsen standing in the doorway.

Mrs. Plotkin turned and sized up Max rapidly. For sure not a bill collector. Too well dressed, and therefore certainly not a parent. She crossed to Max, wearing her celebrated open-school-week smile.

"Is there something I can do for you?" trilling *something*, *do* and *you*.

"Mrs. Plotkin?"

"I'm Mrs. Plotkin."

"Is there somewhere we can talk privately?"

"Right now? I'm in the middle of a class."

"It's about Tippy Blaney." He thought he heard her heart leap.

She gestured past him. "Across the hall . . . the room with the green door . . . would you wait for me there, please."

Max turned, saw the door and headed for it.

There was danger in Sylvia Plotkin's eyes as they swept the classroom. "I'll only be gone a few minutes, so I want absolute silence." Then she turned to Rodriguez. "I'm leaving you in charge, Miguel." His face brightened.

"But I'm warning you, you hear me," waving the ruler like a baton conducting Ravel's *Bolero,* "one commotion . . . one peep out of this room . . . and in the morning . . . deportation proceedings. The rest of you behave yourselves, or I remove all the illustrations from your hygiene books."

She gave them a long, ominous, almost pleading look and for the third time that day inwardly cursed the deceased parents, who had talked her into becoming a teacher.

Max was standing at the window of Mrs. Plotkin's small office when she entered, closed the door, and took a seat behind an inadequate desk, indicating a wicker chair to Max.

"Sit down, Mr. . . ."

"Van Larsen . . . Detective Van Larsen."

Her face fell. "Again."

He sat in the chair and for a moment thought it might tip over.

"What's he done now?" the teacher asked gravely.

"I'm with Missing Persons. Tippy's disappeared. His parents reported it this morning. They haven't seen him since early Friday morning."

Mrs. Plotkin sat forward with her hands clasped. "I haven't seen him since Thursday. I finally phoned his mother Tuesday afternoon. Tippy's cut school before, but never this many days in a row. I thought he might be sick."

"No. Just missing."

(How impersonal, thought Sylvia Plotkin. So dispassionate. Probably the only way to survive in his line of work. Maybe it's the only way to survive in my line of work. Easier said than done.)

"That's too bad," she said, sitting back. "Maybe he ran away. Did he leave a note or anything?"

"Nothing. Just disappeared. His father thinks he may have seen him yesterday at some protest rally in Washington Square."

"That's possible. Tippy does a lot of protesting."

"From your phone call to his mother, I'm assuming you take a special interest in Tippy."

"Well, he's brighter than most. And he has a talent. A kid like that's an oasis in my desert." With a quick move of her head, she indicated the general direction of her classroom. "Across the hall, let me tell you, that's a cultural wasteland."

Max smiled. "They're unusually quiet."

"Those kids are obscene, not heard, especially when Rodriguez is in charge. They're all afraid of him . . . except Tippy."

"Friday morning, before presumably leaving for school, Tippy tried to get five hundred dollars from his father."

Mrs. Plotkin sat up sharply. "Five hun . . . ! Good God! He said he'd ask his father for a small contribution . . . but five hundred dollars!"

Max was lighting a cigarette. "Contribution for what?"

"The kids are doing a show for end of term. You know . . . songs and sketches kidding the teachers, may God have mercy on us. They needed some costumes, some scenery, things like that, so Tippy volunteered to get a contribution from his father."

Max exhaled. "Tippy's weekly allowance is fifty dollars."

Sylvia Plotkin's shoulders sagged. "Had I known that, I would have married him."

Max didn't smile often, but there was something about this plump, wide-open-faced woman that amused him. "And how do you explain that to Mr. Plotkin?"

She waved her hand disdainfully. "I explained that to him five years ago . . . with a Mexican divorce. The hell with it. Water under the bridge." She leaned forward. "What about Tippy? I'm worried. I like that kid." She smiled almost shyly. "There aren't many students you get attached to these days, but Tippy is something else. A little withdrawn, a little suspicious, not overly friendly, too moody at times, but smart." She winked and tapped the side of her head with an index finger. "Lots of good gray matter there. And a poet!"

She opened a desk drawer, pulled out a yellow folder and spread it carefully on the desk. She extracted a page from the folder. "You got a minute?" Max nodded. "Listen to this one. It'll kill you."

Mrs. Plotkin read clearly, enunciating carefully and with pride:

"They're exonerating the Jews in Vatican City,
Centuries too late . . . and oh the pity
Of it all, the millions of slaughtered
Who might have been spared . . . the drawn . . .
the quartered,
The countless ghosts, the bones beneath soil,
Too late in Rome . . . they burn the midnight oil . . ."

She looked up and caught a strange expression on Max's face. "Well, he's only seventeen!" she pleaded. "What were you expecting . . . Allen Ginsberg?"

"Not at all," said Max after clearing his throat. "It just took me by surprise."

"Me too. He wrote it for my birthday a couple of months ago. I almost bust a blood vessel to keep from crying. And look what he calls it." She shoved the sheet of paper toward Max. He leaned over and read "Where the Goys Are."

Max looked up and commented blandly, "Very ironic."

"Wait till you hear *this* one," her voice teasing and enthusiastic. "I dream of hearing him read it at the Ninety-second Street Y."

Max fidgeted in his chair while she leafed through the folder and found another sheet of paper.

"This is the first one he ever gave me. Tippy wrote it three years ago. I was the enemy then. We were all his enemies then. Listen . . ."

There was a brief pause as she rattatatted three coughs, and then she began reading with a lilting fervor:

"Oh teacher dear, your henna'd hair,
Your crossed green eyes beyond compare,
Your big hooked nose, your flaky skin,
Big brown moles and receding chin,
Mountainous breasts and big behind,
And yet I beg you, Be so kind,
Help relieve my one big hurt . . .
To put my hand beneath your skirt!"

She looked at Max. "You're blushing."

His flush deepened. "Weren't you hurt?"

"*Hurt!*" she exploded. "This was the first male to pay any attention in the two years since my divorce!"

Max strained to keep his jaw from dropping.

"You think I got mad when he sent it to me? Like hell I did, Mr. Detective. Don't you understand what it really *means?* Not just the *talent* that's indicated, but the cry for *help!* The cry for *recognition!*" She slammed the sheet down on the desk. "It's the first one of these things I received that *scanned,* for God's sake!" She drew herself up grandly. "Can Bel Kaufman claim better?"

Max laughed. "And that's how you and Tippy became friends?"

"I brought him a collection of poems from home the next day. Dropped it on his desk and said, 'Here, Blaney, you want to be a *good* poet? Then read some of these and *learn.*'" She wagged her head and smiled. "He read them all. Even memorized a few. Three years later," staring down at the folder with warmth flooding her face, "he's still bringing me poems. Only more soul and less innuendo. He's even had some published."

"Who are his enemies?"

"Where?" asked the wide-eyed Mrs. Plotkin. "You mean here? In school? You mean like somebody special? Somebody out to get him?" She thought for a moment. "Nobody I know of, so help me. The majority of my kids . . . they run in packs like the animals too many of them are. But not Tippy. He didn't belong to any gang. He belonged to himself. If that was my kid . . ."

She sighed and leaned back without finishing the sentence. There was a moment's silence before she spoke again. "He wasn't very happy at home, in case you don't already know."

"It's been on my mind."

"That's why I'm surprised about the size of the allowance. I mean he always dresses well and never seems to be wanting for pocket money. I know the father's well off. Never met him, but he sent me that for my birthday." She pointed to a figurine on a shelf just above her head. "At least that's what Tippy said when he brought it."

Max crossed to the shelf and examined the figurine. "Venetian . . . seventeenth century." The low drawn-out whistle was Sylvia Plotkin's. It sounded like a *shofar* being blown in a synagogue. "A very good fake," continued Max. He replaced the figurine on the shelf and turned to the teacher. "But there are those who might mistake it as genuine."

Sylvia Plotkin shrugged. "It was the thought behind the gift that counted."

Max leaned against the wall with his arms folded. "He said his father sent it to you?"

"That's what he told me."

(What a figure of a man, thought Mrs. Plotkin. She was looking at Max and noticing the wedding band. Some women have all the luck. Her eyes moved to the black armband. Maybe the luck's run out.)

"I gather the police have interviewed you before about Tippy."

"None of us are perfect."

"They tell you the circumstances surrounding his thefts?"

"Only that he was a thief."

"Tippy stole some of these figurines from his father's warehouse. His father had him arrested."

The look on her face might have turned stronger men

to stone. "His *own father*? His *own father* had him *arrested*?"

(Wherever you are, Marcus Frog Blaney, mused Max, beware a bolt of lightning sent special delivery to strike you down by an avenging angel of Israel.)

The avenging angel's fists were tightly clenched. "At the time I never asked Tippy to explain. I figured he'd get around to it when he felt like it. But *betrayed!*" Her fists beat the desk top. "By his *own flesh and blood!*" She emitted a long sigh, one part weariness and two parts disgust. "Is it no wonder so many kids today are such a mess? The parents just don't give a damn. Once, when I was a kid, younger than Tippy, my father caught me with a neighbor's son playing 'You Show Me Yours and I'll Show You Mine,' but did he send me to a reformatory? No!" Single fist hitting the desk top. "He took me home and read to me from Havelock Ellis! But today the parents just don't give a damn . . ."

"You don't give a damn! You never did give a damn!"

"I know! I know!" She was out of her chair and standing at the window. "It's the social worker's theme song, but it's true. They just don't give a damn. Poor Tippy. That kid has such guts. He's such a man . . . too soon a man in fact . . . he wouldn't run away." She faced Max. "I feel it in here," tapping the breastbone just above her heart, "something's wrong. He wouldn't go anywhere without coming to say goodbye." She was pensive for a moment, and then her face brightened. "Hey! He has a girl friend! I ran into him a couple of times at night and it was always the same girl! I think she works in a coffee house on Bleecker Street. He introduced us. Now let me think a minute . . ."

"Bibi Something," said Max.

Sylvia Plotkin smiled. "Of course you'd already know. You're a detective."

"Do you have a student named Ashley Tybor?"

Mrs. Plotkin's eyes crinkled into a questioning squint. "Ashley . . ."

". . . Tybor. He collects obituaries."

"Ohhhh!" She laughed. "Whatsisname. The Prince of Darkness. A special name for him. What about him?"

"Mrs. Blaney thinks he's a good friend of Tippy's. If I could speak to him, he might be some help."

"He might," she said thoughtfully, "Tippy's always very nice to him, even if he's a weirdo. Most of the other kids make Whatsisname's life a living hell. Whatsisname. Even I do it. That's what the kids call him. Whatsisname. Ashley Tybor. Imagine saddling a kid with a name like that. I'll send over to the front office. They can locate him. I'll be right back. I got to check the enemy."

Alone, Max re-examined the figurine. Beautiful craftsmanship, but a fake, a genuine fake. He made a mental note to visit Marcus Blaney's auction room.

Antonia Burgess flushed the toilet in the ladies' room, dropped the lid and sat on it, gasping for breath. Twice this morning. Twice those ugly heaves, the dry retching, the searing pain. (I've got to make it through this day, I've got to.) She opened her purse and stared at herself in a hand mirror. She might have burst into tears, but the memory of her mother's voice stayed her. That gentle, lovely voice recorded on a special tape and permanently filed in a hidden recess of her brain, to be played and re-played when comfort was needed.

"You'll be a star, my beautiful Antonia! A big movie star! Bigger even than Antoinette Funicello! You wait and see . . . and see . . . and see . . . and see . . ."

The tape stuck as it often stuck when remorse, self-pity, self-disgust flooded the cell.

(If he doesn't help me, I'll make the bastard pay. As God is my witness, I'll make the bastard pay.)

"Toni? You in here?" The voice belonged to a stock girl.

"Coming," said Antonia weakly.

"Blaney's yelling for you."

(To quote Mr. Blaney, Up him.)

Max figured Ashley Tybor for about sixteen years, maybe fifteen, as he studied the undersized boy sitting in the wicker chair, wearing a black shirt, black trousers, black shoes, enveloped in a black opera cape, and tightly clutching a page that looked as though it had been torn from *The New York Times*.

Ashley's eyes were small and set deeply in his gaunt, undernourished face. His long pointed nose stood out sharply. The tiny mouth looked like a little rosebud, the lips a deep red, almost too lush, too sensuous. The skin was pale and ghostly.

"You're not frightened, are you, Ashley?" Max asked, hoping his voice held the right friendly, paternal note.

"No" came the drawn-out whisper that sent a chill up Sylvia Plotkin's spine. "I'm a bit sad today." He unfolded the page he was clutching. "Did you know Evelyn Waugh is dead?"

Max nodded. "I read about it this morning."

"Too soon," whispered Ashley. Sylvia Plotkin shivered. "I didn't figure him for another four years."

" 'Figure him'?" asked Max curiously.

"I figure everybody," whispered Ashley. "I figure almost to the week they'll die. I don't often figure wrong. I was right on the nose with Sophie Tucker."

Max avoided looking at Sylvia Plotkin. He already had a mental picture of the look on her face. "Is this your . . . *hobby?*" Max asked Ashley.

Ashley nodded slowly. "Sometimes . . . I can pass a person on the street . . . and my eyes meet theirs . . . and I see it . . ."

"See what?"

"The death look."

"Stop that, Tyborg!" Sylvia Plotkin's voice was out of control. Max shot her a look.

"It's my gift," whispered Ashley, "and you cannot deny a gift. Just as Tippy," the whisper now warm and caressing, "could not deny his."

"Tippy is a very talented poet," said Max.

"I am speaking," whispered Ashley, "of his gift for loving. Very few are capable of giving love to others. But Tippy . . . Tippy is blessed. He gives love . . . only" —he paused, looking down at the floor, then back up at Max—"there are so few who know how to accept this love. I"—and he finally smiled, a thin crack of a smile—"I am one of the chosen few." Then his face darkened. "Something's wrong with Tippy."

Sylvia expected a crash of thunder, but none came.

The only dark cloud was the invisible one hovering over Ashley Tybor's head.

"What's wrong with Tippy?" she heard Max asking gently.

"I made a statement, Mr. Van Larsen," whispered Ashley, "I wasn't volunteering information. You're a detective. Tippy hasn't been to school since Thursday. So something's wrong with Tippy. I know. I felt it two days ago. I phoned his mother, but she didn't know where he was either."

Ashley's audience was raptly attentive and he rewarded them with a dramatic pause.

"Then . . . then . . ." in a whisper that would have won approval from Bram Stoker, "the mist drifted through the window into the cellar where I was studying my copy of *Who's Who.*" He stared at the page of obituaries. "I use *Who's Who* in my calculations." He shook his head and sighed. "Watch the papers for Bertrand Russell."

"Ashley," said Max, "when did you last see Tippy?" Later he would wonder why he almost added *alive*.

Ashley bit his lower lip, looked at Sylvia Plotkin, who was making a mental note to meet his parents, then turned to the detective. "Thursday," said Ashley, "in the graveyard."

Sylvia resisted the urge to chew a fingernail. Max's patience with the boy was impressive.

"What graveyard?" asked Max.

"Trinity," whispered Ashley, "on Wall Street. It's very peaceful there. We took a stroll after school."

"Was something troubling Tippy?"

"Many things trouble Tippy. But that particular afternoon he spoke of a desperate need for a large sum of money."

"Did he say why he needed it?"

"No. He was often . . . reticent . . . about his personal problems. Even with me, though we are terribly close. I offered to steal some"—Sylvia Plotkin blanched—"from my father, but Tippy would have none of it. He was so unhappy," a sad, wistful shake of his head, "so terribly unhappy. We mature too soon these days, don't we, Mr. Van Larsen?"

"That kid'll never grow up, Mattie. You're smothering him! Stop being so damned protective. Let him have his hard knocks! Let him experience life on his own terms!"

"How long were you with Tippy that afternoon?"

"A few lovely, precious hours. He wrote a poem in the graveyard and I memorized it. Shall I recite it for you?"

Max knew if he said, "No," tiny cracks of disappointment, and possibly disapproval, would furrow the boy's ashen face.

"I'd like to hear it."

"The search for truth is a lonely search,
Is it in the home? Is it in the church?
Is it in the heart? The soul? The grave?
I must find the truth. I must be brave."

His voice broke and he wept.

Embarrassed, Max turned to Sylvia Plotkin. With a reassuring look she crossed to Ashley and put her arms around him.

"Don't cry Whatsis . . . uh . . . Ashley. Detective Van Larsen will find Tippy. He's only run away, I'm sure that's all. He's just very troubled. I can tell by the poem."

"You don't understand," sobbed Ashley. "That's why I tried to phone him. I've been looking everywhere for him. I have to tell him I'm wrong. Sometimes I'm wrong!"

"Wrong about what?" asked Max gently.

Ashley drew away from Mrs. Plotkin and stared up at Max. "I told him . . . I told him there in the graveyard as he was reciting his poem . . . I told him . . . I told him I saw it in his face . . . and he believed me . . . I told him I saw the death look."

(Now, thought Sylvia Plotkin with her eyes shut, now I need thunder.)

CHAPTER THREE

Lois Corey didn't drop a stitch. She continued basting the hem of the skirt pinned to the dressmaker's model. She had found peace that morning and she would permit nothing to shatter that peace. She had spent an hour in the Christian Science Reading Room and then come home and read two chapters of Norman Vincent Peale, like the cancer patient who followed radium treatment with two Alka-Seltzers. Even while Wilma was telling her about Tippy's disappearance and the sexy detective assigned to locate him, she exuded an air of remarkable serenity. No irregular heartbeat, no rapid pulse, no hot flash, no cold perspiration, no draining of blood.

Peace.

Wilma impatiently jammed a cigarette into her diamond-chip-encrusted holder, irritated by the other woman's annoying serenity. She lit the cigarette, rolled the smoke around in her mouth thoughtfully, then exhaled. "You know where Tippy is, don't you?"

"I don't." Lois bent over, severed the thread with her teeth, pinned the needle to the lapel of her blouse, then sat back with her hands folded in her lap. "Why didn't you tell me about Tippy when I phoned the other day?"

"I didn't want to upset you. Your heart."

"You make more of my heart than I do. Why'd you wait this long before going to the police?"

Wilma waved away a cloud of smoke as she spoke. "You know the family aversion to police. Marcus thought the kid was just acting up again. Van Larsen will probably be around to talk to you."

(I shall remain serene. I shall remain calm. I shall remain placid. I have found peace.) "What does he know?"

"About you? That you're an old friend, Tippy's godmother, you love him very much and he was supposed to have lunch with you on Sunday." She studied Lois for a moment. "You're sure he didn't?"

"I haven't seen him in over a week. The last time he tried to borrow some money. It was a sizable sum and I didn't have it." A wry smile played on her face. "I haven't had a sizable sum in eighteen years. He suggested I ask Basil, but of course I'd have none of that."

"I doubt if your Basil has any of that either."

Lois' smile disappeared. "I don't like the idea of this detective."

"Why worry?" Wilma shrugged. "It's been eighteen years."

"The police have notoriously good memories for facts and faces. The name may be different, but the face is the same." Unconsciously her fingers went to her cheek. "A bit sallower, a few more lines, a wrinkle or two . . . but recognizable. I should have gone abroad the way I had planned then."

"It would have followed you," said Wilma, worrying a cuticle with a thumbnail. "It followed Virginia Hill."

"Poor Ginny," sighed Lois, "she was such a fun girl." The sigh deepened as she stared at the dressmaker's dummy. "I guess Mama knew what she was doing when she taught me how to sew. Wilma . . ."

Wilma was attacking the thumbnail with an emery board. "What?"

"He'd better be all right. Tippy had better be all right."

Wilma's eyes narrowed into slits as they focused on Lois. "Listen you . . . haven't we done enough? He got treated pretty good for a kid who was never wanted. Aaahh . . . he'll turn up. Marcus was right. We should never have gone to the police. The kid's probably home right now messing up the kitchen. And won't he love it when we tell him there's been a dick out looking for him. Won't he just love *that!* Attention . . . all his life he's been screaming for attention! Probably thinks if he stays away long enough, we'll put an ad in the papers begging him to come home and he can have his lousy five hundred dollars."

Lois Corey's eyes were misted with tears.

"For crying out loud, Lois, cool it!"

"He must be in terrible trouble." (Serenity. Peace. Calm.) "Terrible trouble. Five hundred dollars' worth of trouble. Tippy's a good boy. I know he's a good boy!" She beat the sides of her chair with tiny stubborn fists. "If he'd been made to feel wanted, needed, necessary, none of this would have happened. Oh God! God!" She clasped her hands together, the knuckles straining against the skin, agony-white. "Do you suppose he's found out? Do you suppose he knows?"

"You're working yourself up, Lois. Now cut it out! I'm getting nervous. Do you want a brandy?"

"I want Tippy! His is the only love I've had in eighteen years!"

"And what's Basil? The woman's home companion?"

The tears were streaming down Lois' face. "Basil is something else. A different kind of love. Basil helped me to find peace and serenity."

"I wish to hell he was here right now coaching on the sidelines."

"He may never come back."

Wilma was on her way to the sideboard and stopped dead in her tracks. "You have a fight?"

"No."

"Then why won't he come back?"

Lois wiped her eyes with the sleeve of her dress. "He's asked me to marry him. So I told him everything."

"Are you *nuts?*"

"There are too many lies in my life!" cried Lois. "I can't handle any more! He had a right to know!"

"Jesus, Mary and Joseph!"

"When he went back on the road Monday morning, he said we'd talk it out tonight when he gets back. But I don't think he'll come back. I could tell by the way he sounded. And all I have left is Tippy!" She began sobbing convulsively. "I can't lose Tippy now . . . there'll be no reason for living . . ."

Wilma was at the sideboard, pouring a brandy and cursing under her breath. (Complications. There's always got to be complications. I should have avoided this preliminary. Let Van Larsen tackle her and every man for himself. Tippy. Basil. Heart condition. Heart condition my behind.)

"My capsules," she heard Lois whisper, "my capsules . . . sewing machine . . . drawer . . . top . . . right . . . hurry . . ."

The breeze was playing tag with what was left of Basil Kirby's hair. It was too nice a day not to drive with the top down. He hummed to himself as he maneuvered the car skillfully along the throughway. Business had been better than expected. Twenty-two orders for shipments of piece goods. And there had been time to think about Lois and come to a decision, and once he came to a decision, there was no reversing it.

Who she was, a bag woman for the mob, what she had been, that was yesterday's news. What she is now, what she'll continue to be, that mattered more to him. Ten years a childless widower, now nearing fifty—to continue this solitary existence much longer would bring him to the point of no return. They both had a right to expect the best of their remaining years.

As for her obsession about the kid, he'd found the solution to that too.

And that reminded him. He glanced briefly at the silent boy on the seat next to him. He was asleep.

Basil's eyes returned to the road. It was clear and free.

"My family came from Transylvania," Ashley whispered, "they were gypsies. I think that's why I fascinate Tippy."

He was standing in the doorway of Sylvia Plotkin's office, enveloped in his black opera cape.

"I will hear from Tippy," he said darkly. "I know that. And when I do . . . I shall go to him." He slithered across the door sill and disappeared into the hallway.

"I may be Jewish," said Sylvia Plotkin, "but the next time I see that kid, I'm holding up a crucifix."

Van Larsen was sitting on the edge of the desk, staring out the window.

Sylvia folded her arms and crossed toward him slowly. "What was the clue in that poem, Mr. Van Larsen? Which lines tell me Tippy's in trouble? '*I must find the truth . . . I must be brave.*' Is that it? Or am I just reaching?"

The end-of-period bell echoed through the rooms and hallways.

"I'd like to read some more of that boy's poems," said Max. "I think there are a lot of clues to be found in them. He's certainly gone off looking for something. Or else . . ." With a sigh he got to his feet.

"Don't leave it hanging in mid air, Mr. Van Larsen. I can't stand suspense."

". . . Or else he's found it, and it just might have been too much for him . . . or somebody. Have you ever met his parents?"

"Just the mother."

"They don't really give a damn," said Max, "and when I interviewed them this morning, neither did I. But now I'm beginning to."

"Well," said Sylvia Plotkin, wondering if homemade chicken soup appealed to him, "you must get so many of these cases. It must be awfully hard to really feel involved."

"I get more warmth from an ice cube than I get from you."

"Yes. It can be awfully hard."

(Is it his wife that's dead? Who? What? When? Why? How? He should smile more often. He's got a face that makes the lilacs wanna grow. Control yourself, Sylvia. A fresh batch of adversaries are converging on your classroom. And they just don't smile, they laugh in your face.)

"Sorry I took up so much of your time," said Max.

"Will you let me know when Tippy turns up?" Max recognized her concern as genuine. "If you can't reach me here, I'm in the phone book. Plotkin. Sylvia P-l-o-t-k-i-n. Barrow Street. If I'm not home, there's the answering service. But let it ring. By the tenth they sometimes awaken. I think you're a nice guy, Mr. Van Larsen."

"You're a selfish turd! I hate you! The boy hates you! You're nothing!"

"First impressions," Max said and smiled, tipping his hat and heading for the hallway.

When he was gone, Sylvia Plotkin walked to the doorway, hesitated, and listened to the cacophony emanating from her classroom across the hall. She felt terribly lonely.

"There we go!" trilled Wilma. "The color's coming back to your cheeks! Have a sip of the brandy."

Lois sipped.

"You've got to stop giving in to your emotions, Lois. You've got to start being more rational."

"I'm not crazy."

"I didn't say that."

Lois was sitting up on the couch. Wilma sat next to her, took her hand and began rubbing the wrist gently.

"You know Marcus and I have done as much as we could with Tippy."

Lois stared ahead, seeing nothing.

"And when he turns up again," chirruped Wilma, "we'll continue to do as much as we can." Her voice sobered. "But he's seventeen now. He's got a mind of his own. Jesus. *You* were seventeen when you left home, weren't you?"

Lois nodded.

Wilma continued kneading the wrist, establishing a rhythm between her fingers and her mouth. "Tippy's not a baby any more. You know what I think? I think it's Viet Nam."

Lois withdrew her hand. Wilma switched the first-aid treatment to her own wrist.

"You know how Tippy's against war and all that jazz. I'm sure that's it. I mean, he's no coward . . . God knows he's no coward . . . but if he had one, I'll bet he'd burn his draft card or something." She clucked her tongue. "That's part of his trouble. He gets worked up about so many unimportant things. You're the same way."

Lois clenched her teeth together, damming the outburst she felt rising in her throat.

"Now as to the Basil bit," said Wilma, now kneading the muscles at the back of her own neck, "I wish you hadn't been so quick to confide in him. You hardly know the man."

"It's been almost a year." Wilma didn't miss the edge

in Lois' voice. "And when a man as good as he is proposes marriage . . . Oh, what's the use, you never understand me."

"I understand you too well." Wilma's tongue worked like a jackhammer. "And you've always been a very poor judge of character."

Lois sank back, her hands resting limply in her lap. "I'm tired, Wilma. I want to lie down for a while. You better go."

"What about the detective?"

"Don't worry. I've had plenty of experience with detectives."

Wilma got to her feet and gathered up her purse and gloves. "You're beginning to look better. The color's coming back to your cheeks. Finish the brandy and have a little nap. I'll phone you later."

Wilma left and Lois stretched out on the couch. She covered her eyes with her hands and wept softly. She tried to pray, but she wasn't sure to whom and for what. She was too confused. Tippy and Basil and detective were cakewalking through her brain. And the thought that had lain dormant since Monday morning was beginning to elbow its way forward again.

Had Tippy asked Basil for five hundred dollars?

"You are seeking Madame Vilna? You have found Madame Vilna! *Entrez!*"

When she opened the door to her garden apartment in the tired brownstone on East Eleventh Street, Max was startled at how inaccurate had been his mental picture of what the woman would look like. No frail, wizened Maria Ouspenskaya she. Here stood a mountain of a woman, six feet tall at least, two hundred extremely well distributed pounds, jet-black hair pulled back tightly in a bun held in place by a Spanish comb, diaphanous red hostess jacket covering a pailletted yellow blouse, blue toreador pants and green-dyed tennis sneakers.

She held the door wide, beefy left arm outstretched, a magnificent smile lighting up her face, a crescent beauty patch pasted beneath her left cheek, a silver-bell earring dangling from each earlobe and jingling with each toss of her head, which tossed often.

"You are Schwartzkopf from the Workmen's Circle Branch Seven Hundred and Three?"

"I'm Detective Van Larsen from the Police Department."

"Equally welcome, sit down." She slammed the door shut and the house trembled. Max selected an easy chair and sat. He had five to choose from, in addition to three sofas, a love seat, six piles of cushions, two window seats and a hassock. Fortunately, the room was large enough.

"What will you drink? Perhaps some slivovitz?"

Max shook his head no.

"Wine and a *shpritz* of seltzer? Scotch? Gin? Vodka? A chocolate milk?"

"Nothing, thank you. It's a little too early for me."

"I shall sit here!" she caroled, sinking onto the hassock, which emitted a hopeless little *poof* and then expired.

"Now then," with a gay little laugh that conjured up a momentary vision of the Countess Maritza, "the reason why I hit her with the Teflon frying pan and now plead self-defense."

"Hit who?" asked Max.

Madame Vilna jerked her thumb up at the ceiling. "Upstairs. Pola the Polack. To her I am not an *artiste*," eyes smoldering, "I am a *pogrom*." She caught Max's bemused expression. "Are you *really* from the Police Department," wrinkling her nose coyly, "or have you tricked your way in here to rape me? Whaaahhhh ha ha ha!"

It took about fifty seconds for her laughter to subside.

"Two nights ago . . . three doors down . . . Hemingway . . . no relation . . . a spinster lady . . . *raped*. Whaaahhhh ha ha ha," slapping her thighs as the earrings jingled away merrily. "And she *complains* yet!"

There was an impressive transition as the laughter subsided and she stroked her chin, studying Max closely. "You have a *marrr*velous face. I have not seen a face like that since the late Maurice Schwartz in *Yoshe Kalb*. Yes . . . yes . . . there is much pain, much agony, much sorrow, much despair, and a *soupçon* of bewilderment. But of course," indicating the black armband, "you have suffered a *terr*ible tragedy. And therein lies your beauty. Let me see your palm."

"Look, Madame Vilna . . ." Max protested in vain. She held his hand and was studying the palm.

"Yes, yes," she muttered, "it is all there. Great character, great confusion, and you are very passionate." She looked up and winked. "But you have great control, so I am safe." She stared into the palm again. "You have a long lifeline . . . minor illnesses . . . and soon, very soon, you will find peace." She closed his fingers and he withdrew his hand.

"I'm from the Missing Persons Bureau."

"Aha! And who is missing me?" Her eyes twinkling.

"A boy you know has been missing for over five days. Tippy Blaney."

Her eyes popped. "*Tip*peleh? *My* Tippeleh is *missing?*" With amazing agility she leaped to her feet, crossed to the fireplace, rested an elbow on the mantel, clenched the fist and dramatically wedded it to her forehead.

"When did you last see him?"

"Please . . . please . . ." she said softly, "first the shock must recede." She drew in a deep breath, moved away from the fireplace, hands on hips, and paced around the room, head back, staring at the ceiling, miraculously avoiding bumping into the furniture.

"It is im*poss*ible! Tonight we *read!* We read for the Workmen's Circle! Madame Vilna," thumping her chest imperiously, "has never," hand extended and index finger pointing at the ceiling, "*never* missed a performance! I gave birth to my first child during a matinee and evening performance of *Yahrzeit in Odessa*—which you may remember as *East Lynne* very freely translated—and didn't miss a cue! To this day my understudy—whom perhaps you see on television demonstrating cures for arthritis—to this day she curses me!"

She clasped her hands together and beat the air with them in a pumping motion. "But tonight"—she shook her head from side to side sadly, a certain sadness even to the jingling earrings—"tonight I must improvise. La la! There's a first time for everything. Missing, you say. That's not so good." Her face darkened.

"When did you last see him?" asked Max.

"Saturday. Yes . . . yes, it was Saturday. He brought me a new poem. A very *in*teresting poem."

Max was on the edge of his seat. "When Saturday?"

"Ohhhh . . . late in the afternoon. Four, maybe five. Yes . . . yes . . . now I remember . . . he was most distressed." She sat on a couch, legs apart, and leaned forward with fingers interlaced. "He was very much distressed. He needed money, a great deal of money. He said it was not so much for himself . . . for someone else. But look at me . . ."

She hadn't noticed she had Max spellbound.

". . . Look at this apartment . . . this furniture. Old stage props. I am a very poor woman . . . financially, that is. I could not even offer him something to hock." She was back on her feet again and pacing. "Such a talented boy. Such spiritual beauty! So unusual . . . not merely in one so young . . . but in *any*body."

She paused, turned, stared at a ramshackle desk at the far side of the room, and in four long strides, crossed to it, pulled open a drawer, extracted a sheet of paper and waved it in Max's direction. "He told me he had written this poem *that* morning. What it says might be very sig*nif*icant. Vilna shall read."

She crossed to the center of the room and regally drew herself up to her full stature. Her eyes blazed and her nostrils quivered. Max could envision her center stage in a theater, dwarfing her supporting players, commanding attention by the sheer force of the still unabated dynamic personality.

"Like the Phoenix . . ."

Max saw the Phoenix.

"I am risen anew,
Reborn as man and mightier than you . . ."

Her voice rose and fell and crashed against his ears like waves dashing against a palisade wall.

"Ay! Tremble when my shadow falls
Across your path and vengeance calls
To fathers and mothers . . . Betrayers all!"

As she declaimed, she moved slowly to the French doors leading to the garden, and stood almost in silhouette against the sunlight pouring through the dozen square panes of glass, with Max completely hypnotized.

"Betrayers all! Yes, I call you that,
Betrayers of this spawn ye have begat . . ."

She paused. "We had a slight argument about that line."

It took Max five seconds to realize she had interrupted the declamation.

"*Spawn* and *ye* and *begat*." She made a face. "Much too ripe. However . . ." And she began reading again, moving back slowly to the center of the room.

"Assassins . . . Thieves . . . Betrayers . . . Whores!"

She boomed each word as though it had been shot from a cannon.

"Take arms! Take arms! There shall be wars!
I am the enemy! I am the foe!
I sought the truth and now . . ."

She lowered her hands slowly.

". . . I know."

Jingle jingle.

Her head bobbed up and down slowly, still staring at the paper as though hungry for more words.

"That was magnificent, Madame Vilna," said Max. "Thank you."

"I must admit, Mr. Detective, I did not understand it too well on Saturday, but now"—back at the desk, dropping the sheet into the drawer and slowly closing it—"now it has something of a meaning."

She returned to the hassock and sat.

"Now that I think," tapping her head with an index finger, "it is unusual I have not heard from him. Very unusual. Do you know I phoned his mother a few days ago?"

"That's why I'm here."

"Aha!" She laughed. "Perhaps there has been foul play and we are all suspects! Those of us who are presumably his friends. How like *Mishugeneh Mitvuch*, which you perhaps know as *The Cat and the Canary*. Well, Mr. Detective, I am a woman of strange moods and violent tempers and there have been moments when I have been tempted to wring Tippeleh's neck . . . such as when he steps on my lines during a reading, or when he indulges in an occasional petulance . . ." A new thought struck her. "Do you know this unsavory sculptor Clifton Southford?"

"I don't yet, but I will."

"Most unsavory. Tippeleh brought him here once for tea." She shivered and embraced herself. "He is like a ferret. His eyes dart everywhere . . . and where they alight, they devour. I have reason to believe there was a recent unpleasantness between the boy and the ferret. Tippeleh brought him here because he thought Southford might wish to do a sculpture of me. But I said no!" She thumped her chest fiercely. "*Me . . . Vilna . . .* interpreted by a *ferret?* Never!"

She gave the idea further silent consideration, and from the look on her face, Max realized it remained unpleasant.

"It was not the first time Tippeleh sought to assure me immortality." Max looked interested, and Vilna was encouraged to continue. "There was a young painter Tippeleh invited to a reading. The name eludes me but the face remains fresh. A handsome face but with very dark crevices under the eyes. The hair—red hair—it grew down to here," slanting her hand and pressing it against the nape of her neck.

"He made me most uncomfortable and I knew I could never sit for him. Wait!" She leaped to her feet and strode vigorously back to her desk. "I am positive he is in my diary!" She held up a ledger the size of an expensive art book. "I would let you touch my diary, but its heat would scorch your fingers. Whaaahhhh ha ha ha!"

Shaking with laughter, she placed the ledger on the desk, opened a drawer and extracted a lorgnette, which she held to her eyes with a majestic flourish, then opened the ledger and began riffling pages. Max camouflaged a smile with a hand.

"Not him . . . and not him . . . and not him . . ." she muttered as pages flew. "And God forbid not him . . ." Then, triumphantly, "But *him!*" She looked up. "Cardew! Edmund Cardew!"

Max added Edmund Cardew to his list of names.

"I am sure he lives somewhere in our Greenwich Village."

"I'll find him." He placed the paper back in his inside jacket pocket as Madame Vilna returned to the hassock. "When Tippy asked you for the money on Saturday, did he say what it was for?"

"No. It is very strange. I know the boy two or three years now, but in truth, I do not know him as well as I should. I gave a reading at his school once. Shakespeare, Ibsen, Sholem Asch and a sprinkling of Strindberg, which was a serious error. The children were extremely rude. Later, when it was finished and I was leaving . . . most angry, most distraught . . . this boy approached me and apologized for his classmates. That was my Tippeleh and the beginning of our acquaintance. But he gave to me only a small part of himself." She held her thumb and pinkie an inch apart to illustrate. "Just that much. But even that tiny bit was most beautiful."

She threw her arms up in despair. "Why do I speak of him in the past tense? Why do I have this premonition? Do you suppose he has gone to his wars? Met his foes? Met his enemies? And de*feat*ed?" She tore her earrings from her lobes and flung them across the room.

"The parents. What about the parents? Do they weep? Do they show remorse? I have met them and they are unreal. I have been to the auctions and seen the father. He resembles a toad."

(I love you, Madame Vilna.)

"And the mother? *I* . . ." thumping her chest again, I am a *mother!* Four daughters! Three sons! Sixteen grandchildren! And they *adore* me. But she! Mrs. Blaney!

One child . . ." waving an index finger under Max's nose, "only *one* child . . . one confused, ignored, unhappy child. One child to show for her sixteen years of marriage!"

Max grabbed her index finger. "What was that?"

"What was what?"

"How many years of marriage did you say?"

Madame Vilna reclaimed her finger. "I said sixteen, and that is very interesting, isn't it?" She tapped the finger against her chin. "And the boy is seventeen. *Betrayers . . . whores*. Yes, yes . . . the meaning begins to crystallize."

"When did you find this out?"

"From the boy. A few months ago. There had been a party. The parents' wedding anniversary. The mother got drunk. I remember when Tippeleh told me. It is written in my diary. The mother had raised her glass and said, 'Here's to sixteen . . . do we try for seventeen?' And there was of course a fuss between the wife and the toad. Tippeleh came to me the next day and I could see he was troubled." She smiled. "It took a bit of coaxing, but I found out why." She tossed her head with the pride of a show horse. "So I am perhaps of some help after all?"

Warm gestures did not come easily to Max Van Larsen, and he was as surprised as Madame Vilna when he patted her cheek. "I'm very grateful, Madame Vilna. For the poem and for the information."

"If one looks and listens carefully," said Madame Vilna, "every word and every gesture is information." She followed him to the door. "I want to hear from you again, Mr. Detective. I shall not sleep until Tippeleh is back safely." She opened the door and Max stepped into the street. "Perhaps," she intoned, "perhaps he will return . . . when he has risen anew."

As the cab pulled away from the curb, Max leaned forward and said, "Hall of Records."

CHAPTER FOUR

Max Van Larsen's head rested on the back seat of the cab, knees jammed against the front, cigarette smoldering between his fingers though unpuffed, eyes staring out the window but unfocused.

Henry Thorpe Blaney, answers to the name Tippy, but not somebody's pet, just a confused, unhappy boy. Seventeen years of age. Parents married sixteen years, or could that be apocryphal? Had Wilma Blaney been drunk at that party or just a bad mathematician? Last seen by his parents Friday morning after an altercation with the father. Seen on Saturday afternoon by the one, the only, never-to-be-forgotten Madame Vilna. Possibly seen Wednesday noon in Washington Square Park by the toad-frog of a father.

A teen-age boy. Too soon a man. Desperately in need of five hundred smackers, yet the weekly recipient of a fifty-dollar allowance.

Thief and poet. Darling and delinquent. Confused and determined. Contradictions. Always contradictions.

Max jammed the cigarette into the stuffed ashtray in the arm rest. Why don't these bastards ever empty their ashtrays! Now his hands rested on his thighs and he thought of Sylvia Plotkin and a fake Venetian figurine.

The first couple of times he lifted some, I got them back before he could sell them. But then . . . he took one worth over five hundred dollars and sold it for fifty. He wouldn't tell me to who and I had to get it back.

A gift from the father to Sylvia Plotkin, or one the boy had lifted? Why didn't I notice if there was a figurine in Madame Vilna's overcluttered apartment? Were all the stolen figurines accounted for? Or is Marcus Blaney frequently given to sins of omission? Will I notice a figurine in the apartment of an unsavory ferret named Clifton Southford? Or the others on my list?

He removed the sheet of paper from his inside jacket pocket, unfolded it, and referred to the names. Lois Corey, Bibi Something, and the new addition, Edmund Cardew. He scratched his arm and his fingers touched the black armband.

The faces swam up at him.

Mattie and the boy.

He wondered when he could attack the stitches with a razor blade and throw the armband into a waste bin or consign it to an incinerator—and is there such a thing as the death look?

Thursday . . . in the graveyard . . . Trinity . . . on Wall Street . . . it's very peaceful there.

Whatsisname, Prince of Darkness, Ashley Tybor—do you own a figurine given to you by a very special friend? Why do I keep dwelling on figurines? I'm hunting for a missing teen-ager, not a cache of pilfered objets d'art. But is there a connection? Why do my cop instincts tell me there's a connection? Where were my instincts ten days ago when my wife got behind the wheel of a second-hand

Chevy to drive my son to school, and immolated them both in a fiery pyre? The garage attendant's voice. That gravelly voice.

I saw the car going out of control and the kid grabbing for the wheel, but it was too late. It crashed right through the fence and down the embankment, and then I heard this explosion and the flames shot up and . . .

Had her face been too contorted with rage and disgust for me to recognize the death look? What about the boy? But I never looked at his face too often. In his thirteen years, how often had our eyes met or fingers touched? Why after only ten days is it difficult for me to recall his features clearly?

Max sat up abruptly, erasing his wife and son. That's finished. That's done with. It'll always be there, festering in some dark recess of memory, waiting to spring at him in vulnerable moments such as these, but in time it will expire, if ignored. The way the wife and son had expired, also ignored.

You can't ignore Tippy Blaney. It isn't that easy. That kid wouldn't let himself be ignored. He prodded people into an awareness of himself by stealing and loving and writing poetry. The little bastard's a fighter. I want to find him alive.

Why do I think he's dead?

Marcus Blaney stared at the inventory sheets spread across his desk. The fake seventeenth-century Venetian unaccounted for. Three small Dresden monkeys (see no evil, hear no evil, speak no evil) unaccounted for. He dried his sweating palms on the Irish linen handkerchief and scowled at the young man in the brown tweed suit with the frayed cuffs who sat across from him with his arms folded and a neutral expression.

"How come?" croaked Blaney.

The young man shrugged. "I don't know. We've checked and rechecked. They're missing."

"God damn it!" shouted Marcus, slamming a pudgy fist on the desk, "I told you never to let that kid in here again!"

"Mr. Blaney," drawled the unruffled young man, "there's a constant turnover in guards. There are two new ones in the East Room who don't even know what Tippy looks like. And even if they did, it's easy for a kid to slip in and out anonymously with the auction crowds. But then," he added, "it might not have been Tippy. We always have petty thefts. Just go over the insurance lists and you'll . . ."

"All right! All right!" cried Marcus, fanning the air impatiently with his hand.

"Is that all?"

"Yeah. Beat it."

As the young man started to leave, there was a weak tap on the door and Antonia Burgess entered.

(Christ! The way she looks! Why doesn't she go home?)

She held tightly to the doorknob as the young man brushed past her, ignoring the subtly expectant look in her eyes. Her eyes moved to Blaney, his face impatient and inquiring. "Mrs. Yamchack is here, Mr. Blaney . . ." (That's not my voice. That's not the voice Mama once compared to Elsa Martinelli's.)

"Speak up for crissakes!"

Antonia cleared her throat. "Mrs. Yamchack . . . she's upset . . ."

"You're damn right," tromboned Mrs. Yamchack as she swept into the room and slammed a figurine down on Blaney's desk.

Blaney jumped to his feet with a quick smile, rubbing his palms against the sides of his trousers as Antonia left. "And how is Mrs. Yamchack?" he croaked.

"Yamchack fine!" in B-flat, "but this miserable fake," pointing at the figurine, "is a *fake!*"

"Fake?"

"Fake!"

"But my dealers in Italy . . ."

"Screw your dealers in Italy! It's a fake. I had it reappraised!"

"But . . . but . . . but . . ." like an outboard motor.

"Blaney, you just don't argue with my buddies at Tiffany's. They say it's a fake, it's a mother-grabbing *fake!*"

Antonia sat at her desk, rubbing cologne on her wrists, when the intercom buzzed. She reached for the button with an effort and pressed it. "Yes?"

"Toni," said the female voice, "new shipment's in."

"Oh, thank God."

"For what?"

"I'll tell Mr. Blaney."

"Okey doke."

"Wait!"

"Now what."

"Tell Eddie."

Shortly after 2 P.M. Max Van Larsen left the Hall of Records with duplicates of birth and marriage certificates in his inside jacket pocket. He hailed a cab and directed the driver to the Blaney Warehouse and Auction Rooms on West Broadway. He hadn't had lunch and he should have been hungry, but it wasn't his stomach that gnawed, it was his mind.

Perhaps he should have phoned ahead and alerted the frog, but at the moment he favored the element of surprise. Perhaps his newly acquired information didn't bear much relationship to Tippy Blaney's disappearance. Perhaps it was information before the fact, irrelevant, immaterial, and privileged, but what gnawed at his mind was instinct. What flashed through his brain were the lines of a poem, lines written by an adolescent too old for his years:

I am the enemy, I am the foe,
I sought the truth and now I know.

And I know the truth too. If it's the same truth the boy was seeking, then it could be a link to his disappearance. But do the lines of that angry poem apply to the information in my pocket, or is there something else? Documents can lie, but even in lies, there can be a hint of the truth.

The cab pulled up at Blaney's. Max paid the fare and got out as a large woman jostled past him, got into the cab and tromboned, "The Regency . . . and no conversation!"

Antonia stared at Max, her fingers tightly clenching the edge of the desk, her heart thumping wildly. "Yes, Detective Van Larsen?"

(What the hell's wrong with her, Max was thinking. She acts as though I'm about to make a pinch.)

"I'd like to see Mr. Blaney."

Her words stumbled out under the lash of an invisible whip. "In reference to what?"

"His son."

"Oh!" The relief in her voice inundated Max. "I'll tell him you're here." She reached to the intercom.

Max studied Antonia carefully as she announced him to Blaney. The dissolute look of her was a familiar one to him. It could fit one of several classifications, but there was no time now to pinpoint it. The frog was waiting to see him.

Blaney shoved Mrs. Yamchack's figurine into a desk drawer as Max entered, closed the door and sat down. Ignoring Blaney's outstretched hand, he withdrew the documents from his pocket and flung the papers on the desk.

Blaney stared at them. "What's this?"

"Read them."

Blaney scanned them swiftly, and as he did, beet-red colored his face. He pulled at the handkerchief in his back pocket and wiped the palms of his hands. Then, slowly, he wedded his well-upholstered frame to the well-upholstered chair and locked eyes with the detective. "So?" he croaked.

"Did the kid know he was illegitimate?"

"Christ no! What do you take us for?"

"Who's Laura Cecci?"

The frog blinked his eyes, licked his lips, and little beads of perspiration formed on his forehead.

"Any relation to Wilma Cecci?" prodded Van Larsen.

"Her sister." The voice was a squeak.

"So Tippy's your nephew."

"Yeah."

"Who's the father?"

"Like it says there."

"Joe Jones."

"Yeah."

"One of the Jones boys?"

Blaney was squirming. "I don't know who the joker was. Laura never said."

"Where's Laura now?"

"I don't know."

"Doesn't keep in touch? Never curious as to her son's welfare?"

"We don't know where she is. Honest."

"The same Laura Cecci mixed up in that Congressional investigation sixteen years ago?"

"Eighteen," corrected Blaney, then reddening again.

"The same Laura Cecci." Max smiled. "And who was Marcus Blaney eighteen years ago?"

"What the hell do you mean by that?"

"I could put a tracer on you."

Marcus deflated slowly. His skin seemed to sag, almost to the point of shriveling. Instant dehydration.

"Listen," he pleaded, "I'm clear. I been clear since then." (The tear in his voice momentarily brought to Max's mind a memory of that radio tenor who used to shred the airwaves with "Marta, Rambling Rose of the

Wildwood.") "I run a legit business here. It wasn't easy getting started again. I got respect now."

Marcus fumbled with a package of cigarettes. "Laggio." He spoke the name softly, laying a wreath at its feet. "Mario Laggio." The hand lighting the cigarette was trembling. "You really need all this to find the kid?"

Max leaned forward, drumming his fingers on the desk top. "If the kid ran away, I'm trying to figure out what made him do it. I'm trying to put myself in his shoes, in his skin. It helps in my line of work. I try to conjure up mental pictures of my runaways. You'd be surprised at the results."

"Put yourself in the boy's shoes. Just once . . . just once . . . try to see yourself through his eyes . . ."

Max ignored Mattie's shade attempting to jam his circuit. "Tippy's unhappy . . . in trouble . . . but why and what kind? Why'd he need five hundred bucks? For getaway dough? Getaway from what? He wouldn't have advertised his plans by asking you for it. He doesn't like you."

"I been good to him!"

"Not good enough. Maybe he went looking for Laura Cecci."

"He doesn't know a thing about Laura! All he knows is Wilma and me are his parents."

"You're so sure."

"How could he find out?" His arms were outstretched like a peanut vendor explaining a depleted stock. "Who would tell him? Only Wilma . . . only Wilma and me know. Aaahhh, it's like I said this morning. He's staying away just to get us upset."

"You don't know him."

"What? I don't know *that kid?* Seventeen years under the same roof and I don't know *him?*"

"I know more about him in five hours than you know in seventeen years. He's clever. He's aware. He knows he's illegitimate and you know he knows."

"I don't!"

"There was your wedding anniversary a couple of months ago. Your wife got drunk and toasted your *sixteen* years of marriage. The kid goes to school. He can subtract . . . and add. How'd you try to weasel your way out of it then?"

It seemed as though invisible hands were kneading and reshaping Blaney's face like silly putty. "Wilma was drunk. Tippy could see that for himself. I made some joke about it. He seemed convinced then."

"He's also a good little actor, and you're not so hard to fool. When was his last theft . . . that Dresden figure worth 'thousands'? Before or after the party?"

"After. Just a couple of months ago."

"You really give the kid fifty dollars a week?"

"Oh Christ." Blaney slumped in his seat, staring at the lit end of his cigarette.

"How much?"

"Less."

"How much less."

"Five bucks a week."

"Why the lie? You and the wife trying to make yourselves look big?"

"It was Wilma's idea. She's ashamed he's run away. She's been guilty about the way we don't pay too much attention to him. She . . . she wanted it to sound like he had no good reason to disappear on us."

Max was toying with Blaney's pack of cigarettes. "Did Tippy know some of those figurines he stole were fakes?"

"What do you mean *fakes!*" rearing up angrily, praying no telltale wisp of angry smoke would drift from the crack in the drawer where Mrs. Yamchack's figurine was stashed.

"Fakes. Imperfect texture not noticeable except to an expert. Rub hard enough on the inside with your thumb and it gets powdery. I examined one today."

"Where?" Too anxious, too quick.

"I might tell you," said Max, smiling, savoring each word maliciously, "and then I might not. The owner treasures it. Tippy said it was a gift from you. But it's a fake. Good imitation Venetian . . . imported from Italy . . . but a fake."

"Well, you see . . ." Marcus fumbled, a rivulet of perspiration streaming down his temple past his ear. "I get stuck sometimes. You got to figure on getting stuck in this business from time to time."

"Always deal with the same outfit in Italy?"

"What's my business got to do with Tippy's disappearance?"

"I'm wondering myself. He used to hang around here a lot. He may have seen and heard things that disturbed him. Maybe he was finding out things it was better a teenage kid shouldn't know. What about your clientele? Do any of them guess they've been stuck?"

Marcus clenched his fist to keep the hand from

moving to the telltale drawer. "God damn it! I got one of the best reputations in town!"

"And the higher echelon does all it can to make sure it stays that way."

Marcus paled.

"Your *paisanos* do a big business in fakery," said Max, "Fake old masters . . . fake antiques . . . fake figurines . . . fake identities . . ." flinging the cigarette pack across the desk toward Marcus, "fake stamps for smuggled cigarettes. You name it, they're faking it."

The Irish linen handkerchief was back in play again. "I told you I'm out of that."

"That's what you told me," nodded the detective, "that's not what I believe. If I don't get a lead on the boy soon, I may have to put it on the teletype. You wouldn't like that, would you? It might make the newspapers. That'll draw attention to you and this place. And you're one salesman who doesn't want attention to be paid. The boys on top would like that less. That's why you waited till this morning to report Tippy's disappearance. Any way you look at it, Laggio . . ."

"*Blaney!*"

("*Van* . . . Larsen . . .")

". . . By any other name, you're in the hot seat."

Marcus leaped from his chair and crossed to a water cooler. He fumbled for a paper cup and on the fourth try managed to draw one out of the wall container without crushing it. He drew water and swallowed it in a gulp. Max's eyes never left him.

Marcus crumpled the paper cup and flung it into a wastebasket. He crossed back to his desk and sat. "Listen, Van Larsen," a daub of menace tinting his colorless voice, "I'm straight. You hear me, I'm straight. Yeah, yeah, I still do business with the boys, but that's because I have to. This is one club nobody resigns from. But I keep an eye out for the fakes that come in here. That's why I got so upset when I found out Tippy was stealing from me. If one of those things got into the wrong hands before I could verify them . . . well . . . you get the idea."

(I've got lots of ideas.)

"The fakes," continued Marcus, "I sell to the *shloch* shops in the village . . . the tourist traps."

"Sure."

"So help me!"

"And these cigarettes?"

"What do you want from me? I buy cigarettes all over the neighborhood. There's big traffic in smuggled butts going on all over the city. Just because *I* happen to latch on to a pack!" He leaned back, feeling better, enjoying his newly restored self-confidence.

(Smart little bastard, thought Van Larsen. It would take a lot of time to get the goods on you if there are goods to be gotten. And that's not my department, they keep reminding me. I'm tracing a missing teen-ager. The real thing. No fake. An illegal importation, smuggled through a maternity ward, but a genuine article. A human being.)

Marcus reached for a fresh cigarette. "Got any leads on the kid?"

Max nodded as he resumed drumming the top of the desk. "He visited Madame Vilna, Saturday afternoon."

"So he was still around then." Blaney almost looked eager, like a housewife in a supermarket spotting a bargain in a product she never used.

"He was still around then," said Max, "still trying to raise five hundred dollars." A dramatic pause followed while Max searched Blaney's face and found nothing. "You're sure he didn't try to blackmail it out of you?"

"For *crying* out *loud!*" Marcus leaned forward agitatedly, covering his face with his pudgy hands.

"Just trying to figure the kid's motives, Blaney, that's all. Like I said, just trying to put myself in his shoes."

"Try to understand how he feels. Lonely . . . rejected. He's a good boy, Max. He needs you. He's at that age where a father is more important than ever. Will you lower that goddamned symphony and pay attention to me?"

Max had arisen and was heading for the door.

"You're not putting it on the teletype, are you?" asked Blaney in an unsteady voice.

Max turned and stared at the sorry, perspiring creature. "Not yet. Too soon. But I may have to. I'll let you know if it's necessary."

Marcus watched the door shut behind Van Larsen. He reached for his private phone and dialed rapidly.

Antonia Burgess was inhaling hungrily from a vial of what appeared to be smelling salts. Max had a moment to appraise her before she realized his presence. (She looked better once, thought Max, fresh and bright and appealing, if I'm still any judge of women, before and after deterioration. The sallow complexion, the clamminess of the skin, the trembling hand, I think I know what's wrong. Maybe not. Sometimes my radar's faulty. Maybe if I could bring her completely into focus . . .)

Her head jerked up abruptly and the glazed eyes saw Max. He had a brief glance at the contents of her open purse as she dropped the vial into it and snapped it shut.

"Can you spare a few minutes?" asked Max on impulse.

Her hands were on the desk, fingers intersticed too tightly. "I can't help you much with Tippy." Her voice was hard and unreal.

"Who fingered Tippy for the thefts around here?"

Her lips trembled slightly, then she spoke. "The guards."

"Any one in particular?"

"It happened more than once," fighting for control of both voice and body. "Mr. Blaney must have told you that."

Max switched to another channel. "The boy never confide in you at one time or another?"

She shook her head. "He didn't drop into the office much."

"Blaney discourage that?"

"I did." (Go away, Detective, go away quick. The pains are fierce and the nausea's rising again and I've got to survive the rest of these deadly hours. The new shipment's being unloaded and there are the invoices to check.)

"You want me to get somebody?" she heard Max asking.

"For what?" slurred.

"You look faint."

She took a deep breath, fluttering her eyelids in an attempt to brighten the irises, and mustered a smile. "A little under the weather, that's all. Anything else?"

"No," said Max, "nothing else. Thanks." At the door, he turned to her. "A couple of spoonfuls of sugar might help."

She didn't acknowledge the remark and he left.

Then the dry heaves began again.

Max passed an auction room and heard an oil painting being knocked down for ten thousand dollars. He passed several guards and rows of display cases. He passed a well-dressed woman oohing and aaahing over a Swiss music box being shown her by a young man wearing a brown tweed suit with frayed cuffs. He heard the young man mellifluously extolling the virtues of the music box and was tempted to glance at him and did. He saw a handsome profile marred by a deep shadow under the eye and red hair that grew to just below the nape of his neck, and wondered if the *paisanos* had gotten a foot into the Swiss music-box market, and then he thought of Swiss cheese and food and decided to get some lunch.

The table rattled as Wilma Blaney slammed the phone down.

"Holy Mary Mother of God!" she exploded, drawing the flimsy black negligee tightly around her as she crossed to the dressing table and reached for the spirits of ammonia. "Holy Mary . . ." Sniff. "Mother . . ." Sniff. "Of God . . ." Sniff.

Still clutching the spirits of ammonia, she returned to the phone, sat on the edge of the bed and dialed. She tapped her foot impatiently, waiting for the connection.

"Hello?" Lois sounded better.

"It's Wilma. You okay?"

"I'm okay. Any word?"

"No. But listen, and for God's sake don't get upset. That detective's found out a couple of things."

"Like what?"

(Damn, thought Wilma, she's getting tense.) "Now take it easy. Marcus handled him beautifully. He's got Van Larsen going around in circles."

"What does he *know*?"

"Now listen, Lois, we knew some day it might happen, so just take it easy and listen. He's been doing some snooping. He knows Tippy's not our kid . . . Lois? Lois, are you okay?"

Lois broke a capsule under her nose with thumb and index finger and inhaled deeply.

"Lois? Lois?" Then frantically, "Lois, talk to me!"

"I'm all right, I said. Does he know about Laura Cecci?"

"Yes. He knows she's the mother, but Marcus told him we haven't heard from her in years . . . no idea where she is or what's become of her. Now, when he comes to see you, you follow the same line, get it? Lois, are you listening?"

"Yes, yes, I'm listening. I hate what I hear, but I'm listening."

"There's nothing to be afraid of and there's nothing to worry about. Marcus is doing something about Van Larsen."

"Like what?"

"Like seeing to it he lowers the heat. So just sit tight in the meantime and play it cool . . . okay, sweetie?"

"I'll be all right."

"Call me after you see Van Larsen, okay?"

"Maybe he won't come."

"I wouldn't bet on it."

"Okay."

Lois hung up and stared at the dressmaker's dummy. Slowly she withdrew the needle from her lapel. (I am calm. I am serene. I am at peace.)

"Ow!" She pricked her thumb. A tiny drop of blood appeared. She sat quietly, thumb in mouth, looking for all the world like the lonesome, forlorn child she had always been.

(Pain. There's always pain. With Mama, pain. With Tippy, pain. And you, Basil? Pain? Will you use my confidence as a weapon? Or will you come back tonight and stroke my hair, pet my cheek, null my throbbing pains? I'll learn to love you if you do that, Basil, I promise I will.)

"What's the matter kid?"

"Cramped." The boy shifted in his seat.

"We can look for a place to stretch our legs. Maybe a beer. How's a beer sound to you?"

"Sounds fine."

"There's a Howard Johnson's a couple of miles ahead. I'll pull off the throughway when we get to it. Okay?"

"Okay."

CHAPTER FIVE

Max ate less than half of the tuna fish sandwich that tasted too vinegary, drained the cup of coffee, which was tepid and bitter, and chewed two stomach mints. He left fifteen cents for the counterman, handed a dollar to the cashier, collected his change, and strolled out into the street. A few feet from the luncheonette he paused in a doorway and referred again to the list of names.

Lois Corey.

Bibi Something.

Clifton Southford.

Edmund Cardew.

Antonia Burgess?

Too early for Bibi Something if she only worked nights at the Cloven Hoof. He settled on Clifton Southford and decided it would be quicker to walk to University Place. Greenwich Village traffic was hopeless at any hour of the day, and he was in no mood for cramping himself again into an undersized taxi.

As he walked, he thought of the things that still needed to be done in the apartment. Pack Mattie's clothes and costume jewelry and ship them to her mother in

Poughkeepsie. Thin-lipped bitch with the accusing eyes.

"Not a tear, Max Van Larsen. You haven't shed a tear. Didn't Mattie and the boy mean anything to you?"

They had meant nothing.

(I tried at first when she was pregnant, then that year after the boy was born, but I never loved her and I couldn't learn to love him. I can't love anything that's forced on me. I didn't want her and I didn't want the boy. I didn't want them dead either, but I didn't want them ever. What'll I do with the boy's clothes? The boy. Always the boy. Never Derek. Never an affectionate nickname like *Tippy*. Just *the boy*. The thing. *That* sitting over there. That doing his homework. The boy. The unwanted. The boy and his mother. The only clutter in an otherwise orderly life. Was there a time I really thought I could learn to love Mattie?

There was briefly that time when I was walking the beat and she clerked at the bookstore. She seemed to know art books well. Why didn't I know then . . . why wasn't I smart enough to differentiate between knowledge and a good memory? And she said she liked Brahms and Antheil and the films of Kurasawa, and then yawned a great deal when listening to Brahms and Antheil and watching the films of Kurasawa. What a crash course she must have put herself through for my sake.)

One of the few credits he would allow her. And what a crashing bore she turned out to be.

"I won't do it! I won't! It's against my religion!" and then never set foot in a church from the day the boy was born.

The boy. His things. His meager things. Maybe the Salvation Army. Maybe one of those organizations that occasionally canvass door to door for needy children. Maybe . . . maybe Sylvia Plotkin might have some ideas. Sylvia Plotkin. He smiled to himself at the thought of the sweet, spunky little woman: *"I may be Jewish, but the next time I see that kid, I'm holding up a crucifix."*

(Derek.

I baptize thee Derek Nils Van Larsen in the name of the Father, the Son and the Holy Ghost. *Unholy ghost Derek.* What was his godmother's name? Marie . . . Mary . . . Madge . . . Adrienne . . . whatever became of her? Whatever became of all of Mattie's friends?)

"It's you! You're the reason I've lost all my friends. You treat them like dirt. You treat everyone like dirt. What makes you think you're so special? You're just a cop! With all your two-bit intellect and second-hand pretensions, you're just a nothing cop!"

(Epitaph.

What do I tell them to carve on the tombstone? Loving wife and son? Her and That?)

He jumped to avoid a car that came skidding around a corner, and cursed under his breath. He looked at the street sign. University Place.

He pressed the button under the engraved plate lettered: *Clifton Southford, Esq.* He heard the muffled notes of the chimes. They played "Thank Heaven for Little Girls."

Clifton Southford, Esq., opened the door a few inches and squinted curiously at Max Van Larsen. "No soliciting!" snapped Clifton Southford, Esq.

"I'm a detective," said Max swiftly as the door started to shut. "The name's Van Larsen. It's about Tippy Blaney."

Southford pulled the door back slowly. "What about him?"

"Can I come in or do we talk out here in the hall?"

"Come in," his voice crackling like wrapping paper.

Max entered the huge studio with its oyster-white walls, which matched the occupant's complexion, and wood-burning fireplace. In lieu of furnishings, which were sparse (some Eames chairs, a few end tables, a bar and stools), there were dozens of what Southford called his "creations." There was nothing in plaster, terra cotta or wood, not even a sign of clay or cans of tomato soup. But there was a lot of what Max later described to Sylvia Plotkin as "junk and old trash wired or soldered together, and I'll be damned if some of it didn't begin to grow on me."

"Sit down." He hissed the S in Sit.

Max selected an Eames chair. Southford crossed to the bar, perched on a stool, lifted a lit cigarette from what looked like a hub cap (and was), and crossed his legs. He appeared to Max to be in his late fifties or early sixties. He was thin and not very tall, and the closely cropped brown hair seemed to be dyed.

"What's Tippy stolen now?"

Max's eyes traveled the room in search of a figurine, but he saw none. "He hasn't stolen anything. He's disappeared."

Southford threw back his head and a weird rattle that might pass for laughter tore loose from his throat. (A ferret. Very definitely a ferret, Madame Vilna.)

"What's so funny?"

The rattle subsided and only a wry smile remained.

"The last time I saw him, I told him to get lost. That's what's so funny."

"I thought you and the boy were friends."

"We were. I even did a creation of him."

"A what?"

"A creation," his hand sweeping the room with the wrist making dainty curlicues. "These are my creations. That's Tippy over there in the corner. One of my best I'm sure you'll agree."

Max stared at what was purportedly Tippy Blaney. He saw an old alarm-clock face soldered to a wheel that looked as if it had come from a baby carriage. This in turn was attached with wire to a length of stovepipe, at the end of which protruded some drab artificial daisies. The creation was suspended from a hook in the ceiling on a braided rope.

Max couldn't muster an appropriate comment and decided to by-pass an attempt. "When was the last time you saw Tippy?"

"Oh dear. Let me think. I'm so bad on time . . ."

(You're so bad on a lot of things, thought Max.)

"I guess it was about a week ago."

"Did he try to borrow a large sum of money?"

Southford's eyes brightened. "You're psychic!" He jumped off the stool somewhat nimbly, and with cigarette dangling from his lower lip, hands on hips, he began circling Max. "Yes . . . yes, I thought I felt a vibration when you walked past me at the door." Max crossed his legs as Southford stopped in front of him, thrusting his head forward. "You know . . . I think I'd like to do you."

"I couldn't hold still long enough," said Max. "Do you mind sitting and answering a few questions?"

"Most people are flattered when I offer to do them," said Southford with a slight degree of petulance. "For most, it's the one opportunity for immortality. I hang in some of the best museums. Don't confuse *my* creations with the excrement of the Pop-Opportunists."

"Let's get back to Tippy. How much money did he want?"

Southford folded his arms and set his jaw. "I don't remember."

"Was it five hundred dollars?"

"I don't remember."

"Did he say why he needed the money?"

"I don't remember."

"And you had an argument?"

"I don't remember."

Max got out of the chair and crossed to the creation of Tippy. "Would it stimulate your memory any if I tore this from the hook and crowned you?"

"Tsk tsk tsk tsk," clucked Southford, "police brutality. I don't hold with it, young man, nor can I be intimidated by vulgar threats. You disappoint me. Would you like a drink? I've a shaker of very dry vodka martinis. I was about to have one when you appeared on my doorstep."

With a bland expression and an air of hauteur, he stepped behind the bar, poured himself a martini, and still holding the shaker, looked up at Max. "Well? Are you or aren't you martini'ing?" Then, with his free hand, he brandished a bottle of bourbon. "Or would you prefer a suck of Old Granddad?"

"I don't drink on the job."

"You only threaten." He lowered the shaker and the bottle, picked up the glass of martinis, crossed to a chair, and sat with his back to Max. "Do you mind lighting somewhere where you can be seen?"

Max returned to the Eames chair.

Southford delicately sipped the martini, swallowed, ran his tongue around his teeth and then riveted his eyes to Max's face. "When was Tippy reported missing?"

"This morning."

"And how long has he been missed?"

"About five days."

"Have you interviewed that doxy of his, that Bibi somebody or another with the depressing armpits."

"Not yet."

"He wanted five hundred dollars. As a loan, mind you. When I refused, he demanded the return of a gift he had given me a few months ago."

"A figurine."

"Oh God, you're psychic. You're so deliciously psychic. You will change your mind, won't you?" *Pretty please.* "You will let me do you? For starters I see a crankcase, an ice cube tray and a screwdriver. It may sound a bit erotic, but that's how I see you. I have to do people as I see them. 'This above all: to thine own self be true.'" He simpered.

"I'd like to see the figurine."

"It's in the bedroom on my dressing table." Carrying the martini, he crossed to the bedroom. In the doorway, he turned to Max. "Well, aren't you coming?"

"Is it riveted to the dressing table?"

Southford tossed his head and disappeared into the

bedroom. Max exhaled and then lit a cigarette. Soon Southford was back with the figurine, which he handed to Max. The detective examined it carefully.

"Rather pretty little thing, isn't it?" said Southford. "It's an oriole. Delft. I like to think it might once have been admired by Anne of Cleves."

Max plinked it with his thumb and index finger. "Fake."

"Me or it?" Southford said.

"Either or," replied Max, handing the figurine back to the sculptor, who placed it on an end table.

Southford sank to the floor with his legs crossed and smiled at Max. "I knew it was a fake when he gave it to me. I could see there wasn't enough body to it. I can tell when there isn't enough body to things." His eyes ran up and down Max like ten fingers on a piano playing scales. "Tippy thought it had some value. He's been stealing those things from his father. But since it was worthless, I saw no reason to give it back. Would *you*?"

"How long have you known the boy?"

"Aren't there laws about invasion of privacy?"

"How long?"

Southford sighed. "About a year or so. He came to one of my exhibits. He introduced himself and I was quite taken with his clever little ways. One always is at first with Tippy."

"And so you offered to do him."

"Yes, and there he hangs." A sly look projected from his eyes. "And if you think your underlying subtleties have escaped me, you're quite wrong. I'm not gay, I'm affected. I have a wife and two grown sons. My wife lives in the south of Spain." Sip. "With a lover." Sip. "An unfrocked priest." Sip. "Margaret's not a bad sort, if you like Margaret. My oldest son is a Presbyterian minister and the other is with the Peace Corps." He tossed his head proudly. "I've given one son to God and the other to my country. I regret not having sired a third for General Electric. *Now* will you consider being done by me?"

"I'm more concerned with Tippy's whereabouts at the moment. You had a serious falling-out."

"Psychic, psychic, psychic!"

"Madame Vilna."

"That harridan!" He was on his feet again and back at the bar, refilling his glass. "It's like I told you. The falling-out was over that damn figurine. He didn't believe it was a fake. He said his father told him a lot of them were fakes, but he didn't believe that one either. Tippy has something of a talent for believing only what he wants to believe. Like that time with one of my collages in the bedroom."

"What about it?"

"Go see for yourself," said Southford slyly. "It's much too heavy to lift off the wall. I'm so frail."

Max went to the bedroom.

In the center of the room was a king-sized bed illuminated by half a dozen spotlights artfully arranged on the ceiling. Next to the bed was a small table with a night lamp and a pink princess telephone. The rest of the room was piled high with stacks of old magazines and newspapers. The walls were covered with collages of various sizes and dimensions, clever arrangements of clippings from the magazines and newspapers.

The first collage to attract his attention was an artful potpourri of child movie stars and little girls. Shirley

Temple with Sybil Jason and Cora Sue Collins overlapped the Castro child mastering the art of opening one of her father's convertible couches.

"Not that one . . . *that* one."

Max hadn't heard Southford creep up behind him. He was indicating the largest collage in the room, which hung on the wall just beyond the bed. Max crossed to it and studied it carefully. It was mostly snippets of old newspaper headlines and photographs of an array of unfortunate females, again cleverly arranged. The gallery included such familiar faces as those of Ruth Snyder, Winnie Ruth Judd and Ethel Rosenberg.

Max's heartbeat quickened.

One headline contained the name "Laura Cecci." Beneath it was a photograph of the woman. Tense. Drawn. Dark glasses. But still beautiful.

"It's my most recent collage," said Southford, "completed just over a week ago. When Tippy saw it, he absolutely seemed to grow faint. With admiration, I thought, but how wrong I was. He started clawing at that Cecci woman's photograph—if you look closely, you can see faint traces of the tiny ruts caused by his fingernails—but I pulled him away"—he was clutching Max's arm tightly—"before he could do any serious damage."

Max shrugged his arm sharply and Southford's hand fell back. "Then Tippy shrieked any number of oaths and imprecations, in a remarkable display of gutter vocabulary, I might add. I was embroiled in a fury of my own. How dare *any*one attempt to deface one of *my* creations. I grabbed him by the collar." Southford winked. "As you have gathered, I keep myself in excellent shape, and after a somewhat tenuous struggle, propelled him back into the living room and flung him into a chair, where he proceeded to sob hysterically."

Southford's narration carried them back to the living room. He pointed at the chair Max had vacated. "He sat there and sobbed endlessly. I tried to offer him sympathy but he slapped my hand away and jumped to his feet. 'Fake,' he shouted. 'Fake! Everything's a fake! Everyone's a fake! Life's a fake! I hate you!' meaning me, ran out the door, and that's the last I've seen of him. Now really," hand impatiently on hip, "*why* can't I do you?"

"Mr. Southford," said Max quietly, "I've already been done." He crossed to the door and opened it.

"You. Van Larsen!" Southford's voice was sharp and commanding.

Max turned to see a smirk on the sculptor's face. "Mr. Van Larsen," he gurgled, "I think you're the biggest fake of all."

Max walked away from the house rapidly, breathing deeply, clenching and unclenching the fingers of his right hand. How close he had come to smashing the sculptor's face. How close. Almost as close as Southford's final words had come to smashing him.

"Madame Vilna?" purred Southford into the princess phone. "Clifton Southford here."

"*Cossack!*"

"A few choice words of admonition and caution, you *termagant* . .

Madame Vilna clutched the phone with both hands. *If only this was the ferret's neck.*

Southford hissed, "Don't ever, ever again maliciously cast suspicions and aspersions on a fellow human being without being cognizant of all the facts. For future reference and future ears, that so-called altercation between Tippy Blaney and myself was a minor spat of minuscule importance."

Madame Vilna's bosom rose and fell like a steam-propelled bellows as she forced herself to control her temper and the volume of her voice. "Listen to me, *paskudnyack*. What I repeated to the charming Van Larsen was exactly as I heard it from Tippeleh . . . word for word verbatim. You are *for*tunate—I repeat *for*tunate—I did not inform the charming Van Larsen of some of your more *out*standing pecul*iar*ities as described to me in colorful detail by the unfortunate boy!"

"Such *as* . . . ?" in high C.

"To *speak* them would be to *foul* my mouth!"

She slammed the phone down and folded her arms around herself, eyes tightly shut, shaking with anger—anger at Southford, anger at herself, anger at a world in which she knew years ago she had ceased to live, merely exist.

Southford winced as he heard the crash of the phone at the other end of the wire. Slowly he lowered his phone into the cradle, crossed to the bedroom and stared at the collage. After several minutes' concentration it told him very little that he didn't already know. Clifton Southford was a genius . . . and genius is entitled to its rarefied pecul*iar*ities.

Cardew, Edmund.

Max found the name in the phone book and jotted

down the address on Cornelia Street. Then he flipped the pages to the P's.

P-l-o-t-k-i-n, Sylvia. Barrow Street. Max found the number and dialed. One ring. Second ring. If he got the answering service, what message would he leave? Third ring. He started to hang up.

"Sylvia Plotkin."

He moved the receiver back to his ear.

"I repeat, Sylvia Plotkin."

The tone of voice told him that's all there was, there wasn't any more, he could take it or leave it.

"Max Van Larsen."

"Oh, *hello*. Have you found him?"

"I've found a lot of things, but not Tippy." He cleared his throat. "Look . . . I know this is sort of short notice . . . but are you free to have dinner with me tonight?"

Feeling faint, the blood rushing to her head like children skipping in a playground, Sylvia Plotkin groped for a chair. It scraped along the floor as she pulled it toward her.

"Hello? Hello?" said Max. "I think we have a bad connection."

Sylvia found her voice. "Oh no! Not at all! I think it's a very good connection. You said something about dinner?"

"Yes, I did. Can you join me?"

"Oh, why . . . yes, why not. Of course I'd be delighted to. What time?"

"We'd better make it a little on the late side if it's all right with you."

(Any side you like because everything's all right with

me right now I hope you like homemade chicken soup you wonderful man you.)

"Better late than never!" she chirruped.

"Around nine o'clock. That okay? I've got a few more people to look up, then check back at the precinct, things like that."

"Would you like to come by for a drink or meet some place or whatever?"

"I thought we might kill two birds."

(For you I'll kill anything.)

"Are you there?"

"Where's to go?" she sang.

"I thought we might try the Cloven Hoof. I have to talk to this kid Bibi Something . . ."

"Oh, fine! Fine! I hear the food's not bad there." (It's poisonous.) "It's not home cooking," like mine, "but I hear it's interesting." (If you own a stomach pump.)

"Let's meet there around nine then."

"That's a date. Oh, wait!"

(What the hell am I perspiring for? thought Max.)

"Whatsisname's been looking for you."

"Who?"

"*Whatsisname*. The Prince of Darkness. Ashley. He called a dozen precincts looking for you, and when he found the one you're attached to they said you were out, so he phoned me in case I should hear from you, which I have, and I should tell you he's trying to get in touch with you because it's urgent."

"What's it about?"

"He wouldn't tell me. He doesn't trust me. I'm a teacher. But he was *crying*. I've got a number for him. Do you have a pencil and a piece of paper?"

(A clean handkerchief? Did you eat something today?)

Max fumbled in his inside jacket pocket for pen and paper. "Okay," he said into the phone. "Got it. See you at nine."

"Nine." They hung up simultaneously.

Sylvia Plotkin cha-cha-cha'd to the closet and pulled open the door. She pushed hangers aside, examining each dress carefully. Yellow . . . beige . . . Ohrbach's . . . black . . . What . . . Which? Black . . . Klein's . . . basic black . . . string of pearls . . . slave bracelet. (*Kiss me, my fool!*) Black pumps . . . hat? No hat. Maybe a hat. The turban. Better yet, the red turban with the imitation pearl (for *real* occasions) dangling from the center. Dinner . . . nine o'clock . . . Max Van Larsen . . . "I dreh-hemt I dweh-helt in mah-harble hallllsss . . ."

She *ha*'d her happiest, most contented *ha* in years.

Max waited patiently for the connection after dialing the number Sylvia Plotkin had given him. He was whistling between his teeth and tapping his right foot in syncopation.

The voice at the other end sobered him. "Mortuary."

CHAPTER SIX

"Mortuary," repeated the voice.

Max had an urge to hang up. But Ashley Tybor hadn't struck him as the type of boy who indulged in pranks.

"Do you," stifling an urge to burst into laughter, "do you have an Ashley Tybor there?"

"Senior or junior?"

(There *would* be two of them.)

"Junior."

"One moment, please. I'll connect you with the embalming room."

The laughter could no longer be stifled. Max covered the mouthpiece with his hand and exploded. It felt good. The release was exhilarating. He could laugh again. He could ask a woman for a date again (but why the perspiration?). But most important, he could laugh again.

"This is Ashley Tybor." The eerie whisper tickled Max's ear and sobered him.

"This is Max Van Larsen. Mrs. Plotkin tells me you've been having a hard time finding me."

(Clouded crystal ball, Tybor?)

"Oh, thank God . . . thank God," whisper-sobbed

the voice on the other end. "I've got to see you right away. I've just got to see you right away!"

"Okay, kid, take it easy. I'm on the corner of University Place and Fifteenth. Where are you?"

"Delancey and the Bowery. There's a church near here we could meet in."

Max felt a twinge at the bottom of his spine. He had an idea how Caesar felt when he crossed the Rubicon. "Why don't we go some place where we can have an ice cream soda?" (Or would you prefer a Bloody Mary?)

"I'd rather meet in the church. Please."

Ashley described one on the Bowery near Chinatown, and Max agreed to meet him there.

Antonia Burgess sat doubled over, hands clutching her stomach, behind the wheel of her car. The parking lot was less than a city block from Blaney's warehouse, but the walk had taken her almost ten minutes. Tears stung her eyes and burned her cheeks, but the pain wasn't half as searing as the torture inside her.

(Get here, you bastard, get here. Get here, I'm dying. Get here or with my last breath I tell all to the cops.) Her head fell against the steering wheel and she barely heard the right door open or felt the impression of the new arrival sliding quietly into the seat next to her.

With an effort she focused her eyes and saw the face she had once caressed and kissed. "Give it to me, you bastard," she sobbed. "Give it to me or on my mother's grave I go to Van Larsen and tell him everything. Give it to me. Jesus, give it to me."

There was no immediate response.

"I'll go to the cops," she gasped, "this time I mean it. I'll blow it all, I swear to you. *Give it to me!*"

Max counted four derelicts spaced among the pews in the dimly lit house of worship. One was a woman dressed in a tattered man's jacket, with a torn man's derby on her head. Her chin hung on her chest and it was difficult to tell if she was praying or dozing. The other derelicts were men.

One had his arms folded on the back of the pew in front of him, his chin resting on his arms, staring in a drunken daze at Jesus on the cross. The second was stretched out in a pew and snoring. The third and nearest to Max sat under a stained-glass window, straining to read a dog-eared book he held an inch from his eyes. Max recognized the jacket cover, *Valley of the Dolls.*

From where he stood, Max saw no sign of the Prince of Darkness.

"Mr. Van Larsen."

The soft, eerie whisper caught Max unawares and he trembled slightly. From behind a pillar the black-opera-cloak-enveloped wraithlike creature appeared. There should have been a pealing organ crescendo at least, thought Max, if not a clap of thunder.

"Over here."

Max followed Ashley to a stone seat set in the rear wall of the church, wide enough to accommodate two people. The boy's eyes were red from crying and his lower lip trembled. Max patted his arm reassuringly.

"I saw him!"

Max tensed.

"He came to me!"

"When?" asked Max hoarsely. "Where?"

"In the graveyard . . . at Trinity . . . after school. I went there to meditate . . . to think about Tippy . . . and he came to me from out of nowhere. He was suddenly there . . . he was suddenly there . . . weeping . . . weeping bitterly."

Max nodded encouragingly. "Did he say where he's been these past five days?"

"In Paradise."

Max moved to put his arm around the boy, but Ashley jerked away. "You don't believe me."

"I believe you," said Max softly. "You had a vision of Tippy. It happens to many people when someone who's away is constantly in their thoughts."

"It was Tippy himself I tell you! I know it was!"

"Did you touch him? Did you shake hands?"

"He beckoned to me . . ."

Max's fingers were working nervously.

". . . and I started to follow. He kept backing away slowly, and I followed. And then he turned and disappeared behind a crypt. I cried, 'Tippy! Wait for me! I want to go with you! Wait for me, Tippy! I need you.' "

His head lowered slowly, and Max realized that the derelict woman was leaning against a pillar, watching them.

"When I got to the crypt, I ran behind it . . . but Tippy was gone." He shut his eyes, clenched his lips tightly, as his body began to shake convulsively.

The derelict woman was at Max's side. "What's the matter with the kid?" Each word dripped alcohol.

"Beat it!" snapped Max, jerking his thumb toward the doors.

She held her ground. "Takes all kinds, don't it?"

Max flashed his badge.

The woman shrugged. "Just another piece of tin to me, sweetheart. Takes all kinds." She jammed her hands in the jacket pockets and moved away.

"Where do you live, Ashley? I'll take you home."

Slowly the head lifted and the boy's eyes found Max. "Are you my friend?"

"If you can't be a father to him, Max, at least be his friend!"

"Yes, Ashley. I'm your friend."

"Then you must believe me. I saw Tippy!"

"I believe you."

"You don't!"

He leaped to his feet, drawing the cape tightly about him. "You don't! No one ever does! But I saw him! He wants me! I need him!" He ran out of the church.

"Wait!" shouted Max. His voice reverberated through the church. The literary derelict flashed him a dirty look, licked a finger, turned a page, and sank deeper into the valley. Max ran for the doors and into the street in time to catch a glimpse of the billowing opera cloak disappear around a corner.

"Christ!" he exclaimed to himself. "Christ! The kid needs help! The kid's sick!"

"The boy needs your help! He's sick! Sick with fear of you! Stop rejecting him! He's your son! He needs you! Help him!"

At the other end of the phone, Max could hear Tybor Senior breathing heavily as he swiftly repeated the scene with Ashley Junior. When he was finished, the worried father assured him he would find the boy and take him to the doctor for a checkup. He thanked Max profusely for his concern, and when he hung up the phone, it took him several minutes to control his attack of chills.

"Basil . . ."

The pain in the voice alarmed the salesman. "What's the matter, kid?"

The boy was clutching his stomach with his left hand, gripping the dashboard with the other. "I'm sick," he gasped.

Basil was eying an annoying tailgater through the rear-view mirror. "You shouldn't have gobbled those hot dogs."

"Pull over, Basil. Pull over. I have to vomit."

(Oh God, thought Basil, I just had the seats re-upholstered.) "Take ten deep breaths, kid," he urged nervously, "there's an exit half a mile ahead. I'll count with you. One . . . two . . . three . . ."

Lois Corey sat staring out of a window of her ground-floor apartment, watching the teen-age beatniks tying multi-colored Japanese lanterns, balloons, and ornaments to trees and wires strung across the street from building to building.

A block party . . . She smiled to herself. (We used to have those when we were kids. We made bonfires and toasted marshmallows and roasted potatoes (*mickeys!*) and danced Ring around Rosie and sang Row, Row, Row, Your Boat and sometimes Dirty Mary, Will You Get Up, We Need the Bedsheets for the Table until somebody, usually Mama, came running out with a pail of water and doused the fires and made us go inside to bed. There's always somebody throwing water when you're having fun. Always water. Always.

(Don't throw water on me, Basil. I'm not what I used to be. I'll be a good wife, I promise. We'll get along just swell, the three of us, you, me, and Tippy.)

Her eyes moved to the good-looking man standing at the foot of her stoop, studying the faded numbers on the building. (Is that him? she wondered. Is that the detective? *I am serene. I am calm. I am at peace.* I am frightened. Be still, my heart.)

Max caught a fleeting glimpse of the woman sitting in the window before she got up abruptly and moved away. (I know that face, thought Max, I've seen it before. But where?) His eyes moved to the derelict building adjoining Lois Corey's tenement. From a window above a sign that read "CONDEMNED—NO TRESPASSING" a teen-ager was tying a cluster of balloons that looked like a bouquet of phallic symbols.

"Pheee-ew!" yelled the boy to his friends in the street. "What a stink in here!"

Max ascended the stoop, entered the vestibule, found the name "L. Corey," and pressed the buzzer next to it.

Nothing.

He pressed again.

Finally . . . click-click-click.

He pushed the door open, entered the hall and sniffed. Pot roast. Sauerkraut. Urine.

She was standing in her doorway.

"Miss Corey?"

"Yes." She said it sweetly, a hint of a melodious lilt to it.

"I'm Max Van Larsen. Detective Van Larsen."

Her head bobbed up and down as she motioned him to come in. "I thought it was you. I saw you from my window. Wilma told me to expect a visit."

Max entered the room, which was simply but tastefully furnished, and somehow, he thought, too tidy for a dressmaker. There were no snippets of dress material on the floor as he thought there would be, no filaments of thread dangling from her dress, no pile of garments on the chairs or sewing machine. There was an unfinished skirt pinned to the dressmaker's dummy, but even it looked exactly right. He took a seat near the window and from the corner of his eye noticed the pamphlets spread on the table next to him. (Christian Science, he thought, wouldn't you know.)

"Would you like some tea?" Max shook his head no. "Some brandy perhaps?"

"Nothing, thank you."

She sat on the couch and primly pulled at her skirt, then folded her hands in her lap and waited for him to make the next move.

"Have we met before?"

Lois made a production of studying his face and then shook her head. "I don't think so. You don't look at all familiar." She smiled and it was a good smile. (If she gave her face a chance, thought Max, it could be extremely attractive.) "Terrible, isn't it," she said huskily, "this thing with Tippy."

"These things are never very pleasant." He was holding his pack of cigarettes. "Mind if I smoke?"

"Please do."

He lit up and dropped the match in a ceramic ashtray, almost a twin to his back at the office. He resisted the urge to examine it closely.

"That was a gift from Tippy," he heard her say.

"Nice," said Max. "I've got one like it." (What's with the small talk? he admonished himself. Get down to it. She's probably a hell of a lot closer to the kid than those *ersatz* foster parents. Why am I treading on eggshells?)

"She's not well. She's terribly high-strung. And she has a heart condition."

To Max, she looked perfectly calm, perfectly serene, very much at peace with herself. Must be the pamphlets. They had worked wonders on his aunt back in Minnesota, right up to the day she put her husband's shotgun in her mouth and pulled the trigger.

"You're Tippy's godmother."

"Yes."

"Mrs. Blaney" (do *you* know the truth?) "told me you're very close to him."

"I love the boy."

"Have you any idea why he'd do a thing like this?"

She leaned forward, riveting her eyes to his face. "Are you sure he disappeared voluntarily?"

"I'm not sure about anything yet. But why not voluntarily? What makes you suspect otherwise?"

She lowered her head. "I don't know. I'm not sure. He

was so terribly agitated the last time I saw him. He needed money. Desperately."

"Did he say why?"

She shook her head.

"You know the boy has a record of theft."

She nodded, lacing and unlacing her fingers.

"This time he might have stolen money that needed replacing. Have you thought of that?"

She looked up sharply. "He never stole deliberately. It was to annoy Marcus . . . Mr. Blaney . . . his father. Marcus didn't have to be so mean about it!"

(Control, control, thought Max, don't work yourself up to an attack. I've already had a rough afternoon. I saw a teen-age boy cracking up right in front of my eyes. I didn't know such things happen to kids. At least in my presence they haven't. I don't understand kids. I never did till now. And I'm just a beginner. A little late, perhaps . . .)

"It was just a lot of junk," continued Lois feverishly, "and Tippy knew it was junk. He used to spend a lot of time at the auction rooms until Marcus had him barred. Tippy liked the business. He wanted to learn it. He thought that would please Marcus. Tippy told me it was all a lot of junk and I believe him!"

"Some of that so-called junk turned out to be worth a lot of money. It's in Tippy's record."

"It wasn't Tippy's fault. Some good stuff was mixed with the junk. Marcus doesn't always check the shipments. He leaves that to his assistant."

(Interesting, thought Max, very interesting. Could that be the handsome profile with the dark shadow under the eye, the brown jacket with the frayed cuffs?)

"And besides," her voice up an octave, "where would Tippy lay his hands on five hundred dollars? The auction money is kept in a safe in Marcus' office. Even if Tippy found out the combination, he could never get to it undetected!"

"There are ways of entering a warehouse at night."

"He's not a criminal!"

(Stop getting all worked up, lady, for crying out loud. This isn't a television soap . . .) Abruptly he abandoned his thoughts and studied her carefully. So familiar. So very familiar. Her fingers were tightly clasped together and her head was lowered again. Her lips were working as though she were talking to herself.

God give me the strength to remain calm, serene, at peace.

She looked up, and Max thought to himself, with an inner sigh of relief, that she looked almost beatific. Her hands now lay in her lap palms upward and Max half expected to see the stigmata.

"How long have you known the Blaneys?"

"A long time. I've lost count." Her voice was controlled again.

Max took a deep breath and then plunged. "As far back as when the name was Laggio?"

(Here it comes, she told herself, here it comes. Take it easy. It's going to hit the fan. It can all be sidestepped if you're shrewd and take it easy.) "Yes." That came out easily. No flinching. "Wilma and I were friends before she met Marcus."

"Did you know Wilma's sister Laura?"

She managed a wistful smile. (Lillian Gish in *Broken Blossoms*, thought Max, but without the aid of a finger at each corner of the mouth.) "I haven't seen or heard from Laura in years."

"You know the boy's her son."

"Of course."

"Why was it kept from him this long?"

The muscles in her jaw tightened and her voice turned harsh. "Would you like being told your mother used to bed down with a killer . . . that is," catching herself, "a man involved in the rackets."

"Joe Jones?"

Her face betrayed no emotion. Max tapped some ashes into the tray.

"I remember that investigation pretty well. I don't remember any Joe Jones. The name was just a convenience for Tippy's birth certificate, wasn't it?"

(Stay shrewd, she cautioned herself, stay shrewd. You know how to handle cops.) "I've never seen Tippy's birth certificate."

Max stubbed out the cigarette as he spoke. "I'm surprised the Blaneys didn't work up a phony birth certificate with their names as parents. It's been done before if you have the right connections."

Or did they? he wondered. Did they . . . just for Tippy? He thought of Wilma's description of the chaos in Tippy's bedroom. Anger, or had he been looking for something? He's almost of military age. He'd need a birth certificate. Something was gnawing at Max again. Something was telling him Tippy did something or was planning to do something that required a birth certificate.

"I never pried into their private affairs," he heard Lois saying. Outside, the kids decorating the street were getting noisier. He stared out the window.

"Block party?"

"Yes," she said. "They're raising money to stop the war in Viet Nam . . . something like that. They're expecting Joan Baez to appear. It's dress-up." (Well, that's what we called it when we were kids. Dress-up.) "You know . . . costumes . . . masks . . ."

(And beer and cheap booze, Max added to himself, and free love and pot and I feel very sorry for the cops on this beat tonight.) He turned to Lois Corey. "Tippy was supposed to have lunch with you on Sunday."

"He didn't show."

(*Show*. Not *come* or *arrive* or even *turn up*. *Show* is a hard word for a lady like you, lady.) "Did he phone to let you know he wasn't coming?"

"No."

"Has he ever done that before?"

"No. I was disappointed, but it didn't worry me until Monday. That's when I phoned Wilma and she told me they hadn't seen him since Friday morning. Wilma convinced me Tippy was staying away just to annoy them." She moved her right arm to the couch arm and toyed nervously with a piece of fringe. Her head was lowered at an angle and it bugged Max.

(I've seen that face before. It was a much younger face then. There were less lines, less wrinkles, and the mouth was less drawn. I wonder if she's got a record.) "Have you always lived in New York?"

"Yes," she replied, sounding a little annoyed, "I was born in Canarsie."

"Any family?"

Thoroughly annoyed. "What *difference* does it make? What good are all these questions? Is this how you dicks"

(*dicks!*) "look for a missing kid? What's me or my family got to do with it? Or the fact that Wilma and Marcus aren't his real parents? All that matters is he's missing and I want you to find him, do you hear me? I want you to find him!"

"Okay . . . okay, take it easy. I don't mean to upset you. I know you're not well . . ."

"That's right," she cried, "I'm not well!" With an effort she got to her feet. "I have to rest now. You'll have to go. I have nothing else to tell you." She was at the door, holding it ajar.

(Good figure, appraised Max, hell of a good figure for a broad her age. Forty what. One . . . two . . . three . . . maybe not even that. She could pass for younger if she wasn't so tense and drawn. *Tense and drawn.* I saw a face like that today that was tense and drawn.)

"Well, just don't stand there staring at me like I was some kind of a nut case," she shouted. "This is the way out, now take it!"

Max drew in his breath and then enunciated the name clearly. "Laura Cecci."

She slammed the door shut and stood against it, trembling, blood draining from her face, breathing heavily. "Bastard," she whispered, "rotten bastard." With a small moan her eyes closed, and she slid to the floor in a dead faint.

CHAPTER SEVEN

Basil Kirby stared at the knife with astonishment and disbelief. "Put it away, kid, and I'll forget this ever happened."

"It's happening, Basil. And I'll use it if I have to."

The salesman had never heard a voice with such ugly menace.

I shall stay calm. I shall be serene. I shall behave peacefully.

"I thought we were friends, kid."

"I like you fine, Basil. You're a good guy. You'll make Lois a fine husband. And you'll make me a little richer. Throw your wallet on the front seat."

Basil cursed himself for having pulled into this lonely lane.

"Come on, Basil," the boy urged, coloring the menace in his voice, "throw your wallet on the front seat."

"Okay, kid."

He fumbled in his breast pocket and pulled out the wallet. For a brief moment he entertained the thought of hurling it in the boy's face and then lunging for the knife. The boy stepped back as though having read his mind.

"Stop stalling, Basil."

Basil threw the wallet on the front seat.

"Now move back, Basil."

Basil moved back.

"More, Basil. A little more."

Basil moved back a little more, and just as the boy had been measuring to himself, took the one step backward that sent him toppling into a ditch.

The boy jumped into the car, slid behind the wheel, turned the key, moved the shift, gunned the motor, and backed out of the lane.

For sixty stunned seconds Basil remained on his back. Then, hearing the car backing out, he got to his feet, scrambled out of the ditch, and went rushing down the lane to the main road, yelling "Police! Police!" at the top of his lungs.

And God finally smiled fondly on Basil.

A New Jersey patrol car was cruising in his direction.

"Tippyyyyyy . . ."

The whisper drifted through the fetid air of the derelict building, ricocheted and then expired in a dark corner behind one of the many empty packing cases on the top floor.

The Prince of Darkness was huddled in a corner of the old loft with his knees pulled up to his chest.

"I'm coming, Tippy . . . I'm coming . . ."

He was impervious to the rancid odor, impervious to the noise of the youngsters outside decorating the street, impervious to everything but his need for Tippy.

("This is our castle!" Tippy had said that day three

years ago when they first broke into the old building. "I'm Prince Valiant and you're Merlin the magician. Don't tell the other kids about this place. We can hide things here. Leave secret messages for each other. And when we get hungry, there's always Aunt Lois next door!")

"I have your message, Tippy. Give me courage." He wiped his tear-stained cheeks with a dirt-stained hand. *"Give me courage."*

The water dribbled down the sides of Lois Corey's mouth and her eyelids fluttered. Max placed the glass of water on the floor and began chafing her wrists.

(Come on, sweetheart, come on, come to. I don't need any stiffs on my hands right now. Have a heart, baby—your goddamned heart, baby—open those eyes, rejoin the living.)

She opened her eyes. Slowly Max came into focus. Lois pulled her hand away and wiped her mouth. "Bastard," she whispered, "rotten bastard."

Relief flooded Max's face and he lit a cigarette. The chair creaked as he shifted his weight. Lois struggled to a sitting position.

"Can I get you something?" asked Max.

"Yourself out of here."

"Do you want me to call your sister?"

"I don't need anything. I only fainted." She pulled a handkerchief from her dress sleeve and dabbed at her face. She readjusted her dress and then spit the words. "Get the hell out of here."

Max crossed his legs. "I can't find Tippy unless you help me."

"You seem to be doing all right on your own." The color was coming back to her cheeks and there was vinegar in her voice.

"Does Tippy know about you?"

She shoved the handkerchief back into her sleeve. "Does he?"

"Yes."

"When did he tell you?"

"Sunday."

"Then he did come for lunch." His heart was pounding.

"Yes. But he didn't eat."

"Why'd you lie about it?"

"Because I promised him."

"Where is he?"

"I don't know."

"Did he say where he was going when he left you?"

"No. He said he'd call me later that day. He didn't. Maybe back to the house for his things. His box."

"What box?"

"Candy box. An old tin candy box. I gave it to him years ago . . . when candy was important to him."

"What's so important about the box?"

Her eyes flashed. "I gave it to him, that's what's so important!"

"What did he keep in the box?"

"His treasures." Her eyes were misting. "Mostly his poems, I think."

"Then you *knew* he was planning to run away! Why'd you keep it from everybody?"

"To give him a head start, why the hell do you think!"

"Where was he heading?"

"I don't know."

"You're lying."

"So arrest me."

"Have you heard from him at all since Sunday?"

"No."

"Don't lie to me!"

She pushed her hair back. "I'm not lying. I should have heard, but I haven't. He had to get that money first. He couldn't go away without getting that money."

"What was it *for?*"

"He wouldn't tell me." She shook her head sadly. "All of a sudden . . . he got old. He wasn't a kid any more. He happened to see a picture of Laura Cecci some place . . . and he grew old."

"I saw the same picture."

Max told her about the collage in Clifton Southford's bedroom. She struggled to her feet, crossed to the window and stood there looking out.

"They're lighting the fires," she said calmly, "they're getting ready for a good time. He'd be out there with them enjoying himself if it wasn't for . . ." Her voice broke and she wept softly.

"For God's sake, is it my fault the kid can't make friends? What am I supposed to do? Threaten the neighbors with arrest because the kids won't play with the dummy?"

"He's not a dummy! Don't you call him that!"

The room was clouded with Max's cigarette smoke. "Didn't he give you an inkling of what he was planning to do?"

Lois now stood with her back to the wall. She fumbled for the handkerchief and dried her eyes.

Max waited patiently for her to speak.

"He wanted to leave school and enter the service. He'd torn the house apart looking for his birth certificate on Friday. When he couldn't find it, he used his head and went to the Hall of Records. You know what he found out there. Then he went to the Forty-second Street library and they ran him microfilm copies of the *Times* and the investigation. Then he knew it all. When he came here Sunday, we had a nice old-fashioned confrontation . . ."

She sank into a chair and stared at the floor. "He wanted my written permission to join the Navy. I wouldn't give it to him. And I knew he wouldn't ask Marcus." She looked up with a half-smile. "Just think. If he'd have asked Marcus on Friday, Marcus probably would have given him the phony birth certificate and that might have been that."

"The Navy won't take him," said Max, "not with his record."

"He would have thought of something." Lois smiled. "You got to get up real early to outsmart that boy."

"What about his real father?"

Her voice hardened. "What about him?"

"Didn't Tippy want to know about him? Maybe that's who he's looking for."

"His father's in Italy last I heard."

"One of the *paisanos*?"

Her silence said more than a dozen words.

"Are you in touch with him?"

"No!"

"How about Marcus?"

"I don't know."

"How much does Tippy know about Blaney's operation?"

"I don't know what you're talking about."

"His fronting for the *paisanos.* Come on!"

"I don't know anything about that."

"Do you know what Tippy did with the money he got for trading those figurines?"

"He never sold them. He gave them away."

"I can't stop the boy from giving his things away. He thinks that's the way to make friends."

"Marcus told the police he sold some."

"Marcus." She spit the name. "There are those who trust him and there are those who don't. I don't. I gave Tippy to Wilma because there was no other out at the time. They hit me with a year and a day and I was six months pregnant. I had to wear that big coat all through the trial to hide it. At least they kept me under guard in a nursing home so the kid wouldn't be born in the pen.

"Then Wilma took him. She didn't want him but she took him. She owed it to me. Talked Marcus into accepting him when they got married. Then, he'd do anything Wilma told him. Wilma knows how to handle. She handles good. She grew to like Tippy in her way. But Marcus never did. I'd have taken Tippy back when I got out, but the newspapers started playing me up big again. I didn't think the boy had a chance with me for a mother. So I became Aunt Lois."

"Tippy *must* know what goes on behind the scenes at

the warehouse," Max insisted. "That's why he wasn't afraid to help himself to the figurines."

Lois snorted. "He had help."

The detective's temples throbbed. "Who from?"

"I'm not sure." Her voice sagged. "I'm just guessing. Someone who works there. Someone who kept the genuine articles for himself and fobbed the fake ones off on Tippy."

"Why didn't Tippy name him when he was arrested?"

"Because he's loyal, damn you, loyal. That's what the other fink probably counted on. Whoever it is knew if the boy got caught, Marcus wouldn't prosecute. Maybe just teach him a lesson, but never prosecute. I almost *killed* Marcus when he had Tippy arrested those times! I told him Tippy was just being used, but Marcus always discounts what I have to say. And the boy's lips stayed sealed. That's something in this day and age, isn't it? *Loyalty!* And Tippy persisted in believing they were all fakes. He believed what Marcus did to him was Marcus being his own Judas self!"

"Tippy tried to get a figurine back from Southford."

"When?"

"Last week."

She shook her head sadly. "Use your head, Detective. He needs five hundred dollars. So he thinks maybe Marcus was right after all. Maybe some of those figurines are the real thing after all. You get desperate when you need money real bad. Ask me! Ask the kid who knows! So he tries to get one back. It's not so hard to figure."

"No," agreed Max, "not hard to figure at all . . .

now." He stubbed out the cigarette and got to his feet. "You okay?"

"I'm *rotten!*"

Max had the door open.

"Detective!"

He turned and saw anguish in her face.

"Find him. Find him alive."

"I'm doing my best."

She turned away from him. He shut the door and went out into the street.

Max looked at his wristwatch. A few minutes past seven. There was still time to look up Edmund Cardew before meeting Sylvia Plotkin, check back at the precinct, and then maybe home to change his suit.

The street was beginning to look like Coney Island during Mardi Gras. There were hot-dog vendors and pizza vendors and pretzel vendors and beatniks of all shapes, sizes, denominations, and beards beginning to converge on the street. There were even signs of a full moon to heighten the decorations.

He referred to the list of names, committed Cardew's address to memory, and descended the stoop.

Lois watched him leave from her window.

Sprawled on the front seat of the car, the body looked like an abandoned marionette. The right hand, hanging limply, touched the floor. The left was twisted under the back. The legs were jammed under the steering wheel. The head hung over the seat at a grotesque angle, with the eyes open, the tongue protruding from the mouth.

"Looks like her neck was broken," said one patrolman.

The other was rummaging through a purse. He found a driver's license and read the name aloud. "Antonia Burgess."

He turned to the little man leaning against the car parked next to Antonia's, trying not to be sick. "You know her?"

"Officer," squealed the little man, "I just came in here to get my car. There's no attendant here after five. I just happened to look in her car and saw her sprawled there. I thought she was drunk or asleep. When I saw her eyes, I knew better. All I did was my duty as a citizen and went looking for you. So why should I know her?"

The siren on the patrol car screamed a warning at every vehicle in its path. From the back seat, Basil looked through the windshield, eyes glued on the speck half a mile ahead he knew to be his car.

(That crazy kid. That stupid crazy kid. At the speed he's going, he'll wreck the damn car.

Good Samaritan. Every time I try to do something nice for somebody, something like this happens. Lois will never understand this. I know I don't.)

In the loft of the derelict building, the Prince of Darkness lay stretched out on the floor between two old packing cases. His right cheek rested against one of the cases. He was whimpering in his sleep.

Wilma Blaney was giving herself a pedicure and wondering several things in rapid succession. She wondered when the hell Marcus was getting home and what was there in the freezer with which to feed him that she could pop into the oven without defrosting. She wondered if the detective had been to see Lois Corey, and if he had, why hadn't Lois phoned. She wondered what the detective would be like in bed but didn't want to delve too deeply into that wonder and build herself an appetite she knew couldn't be appeased except by Marcus Blaney and she'd rather starve. She wondered what would happen if Tippy was found dead and there was the funeral and what would she wear and would Lois drop dead or break down and spill the beans and would that mean the newspapers again.

Marcus Blaney sat in his office by the light of a solitary lamp, trying to concentrate on the ledger in front of him, cursing first his assistant and then Antonia Burgess. He was waiting for the telephone to ring, the very private one in his bottom drawer constructed especially for very private telephones, and word to reach him that Max Van Larsen had been "contacted" and warned to "lay off." He hoped Van Larsen frightened easily.

Tybor Senior was dialing the Missing Persons Bureau to report a lost son.

Madame Vilna was listening to Tippy's substitute, a last-minute recruit out of desperation, monotonously intoning one of Tippy's (*Tippeleh!*) poems, and knowing in her warm, ample heart that this evening at the Workmen's Circle would be a disaster.

Clifton Southford was stretched out on his bed stark naked, holding to his face a little girl's undergarment, sniffing it, kissing it, writhing in ecstasy, adoring his pecul*iar*ity—and why doesn't everybody?

Sylvia Plotkin stood at the ironing board in her kitchen, carefully pressing her basic black dress, singing "La Cucaracha" at the top of her lungs because Spanish songs had become her specialty since transferring to Robert Wagner High School and she wanted the majority of her students to know she was on their side.

A dozen strides away from Lois Corey's tenement, a perplexing frustration and a sinking depression held hands in Max Van Larsen's mind. For the better part of the day he'd been moving around Greenwich Village accompanied by a phantom boy. An ordinary, dull, routine assignment had grown larger than life, taken on a grand design, and reached him, touched him, moved him as nothing had reached, touched or moved him since he'd been a small boy.

Henry Thorpe Blaney.

(*Derek Nils Van Larsen.*)

Tippy. Bastard. Thief. Poet. Shrewd. Loyal. Deceptive. Loving. Childish. Brave.

(Tippy Blaney, I'm beginning to love you as I should have loved my own son. *I should have loved my own son.* Maybe you're dead, Tippy. Maybe you're alive. Whatever. I want to find you, hold you, comfort you, or mourn you. Cold or warm. Is there someone who will understand this? Or is it enough that I understand?)

Max popped two tablets in his mouth.

The man seated behind the wheel of the armored truck, which bore false license plates, trailed Max Van Larsen for six blocks and cursed under his breath when the detective stopped in front of a brownstone and then entered. At least he doesn't seem to be aware he's being tailed, thought the man seated behind the wheel as he applied the brake and reached for the copy of *Playboy* on the seat next to him.

The woman who opened the door was a handsome Negro in her mid- to late-forties according to Max's rapid calculation. To her quizzical "Yes?" Max flashed his badge.

"I'm Detective Van Larsen of Missing Persons. Is Mr. Cardew in?"

Her unwavering poise in the face of the flashing badge alerted Max that here again was Mother Earth.

"No, he's not," responded the woman. "I'm his cleaner. Sometimes he works late. I don't see him too often. I'm usually out of here by now, but I was late getting started today."

"Do you mind if I come in and wait for him?"

She hesitated for a moment. "Well, I don't know. He's

always told me never to let anyone in unless he's around. He's very particular about his privacy."

"Perhaps you could wait with me."

Her brows furrowed. "Well, I don't know about that. I've got a family that needs feeding and the shopping to do first and . . . I guess a few more minutes won't do me any harm." She stood aside and Max entered.

The room was beautifully decorated and in the ceiling there was an impressive skylight. There were at least thirty or forty paintings hanging on the walls, all tastefully framed, and not many of them, Max mused, very good. He sat in a canvas chair which had "Genius" lettered on the back of it, and lit a cigarette. The woman sat in a straight-backed chair with her hands folded in her lap.

"It's a nice place, isn't it," she said politely.

"Very nice," agreed Max. "He must be a very successful painter."

She considered this for a moment and then spoke. "Well, I used to think that too when I first came to do for him just before Christmas, but he does have a steady job."

"Where does he work?"

She flashed a delightful smile. "I really don't know! We ladies don't ask questions. We just do our job and collect our dollar and a half an hour plus carfare."

"You come here every day?"

"Three times a week, four hours a day."

Max did some fast arithmetic and decided Edmund Cardew must hold down a good job.

"When you do see Mr. Cardew, does he occasionally have any friends with him?"

"He doesn't seem to have many friends if you're judging by me."

"Ever meet a teen-age boy named Tippy Blaney?"

"Oh yes," she said, laughing. "Little Tippy. All spit and ginger that boy. He gives better than he gets sometimes."

(That's the story of his life, lady.) "You heard them arguing?"

"Oh, not really arguing." Her nose crinkled. "Sort of friendly little spats. About art and things. He used to tell Mr. Cardew exactly what he thinks of Mr. C's paintings, and was he honest! How that rags Mr. C!"

"Do you remember when you last saw Tippy here?"

She puffed up her cheeks as she thought. "Oh, I guess not for weeks and weeks."

(Blind alley.) "Real nice place," said Max, rising. "Mind if I look at the rest of it?"

"Well, there's only this and the bedroom." A thought began worrying her. "You're not going to look through drawers and things like that, are you? Because if we leave before Mr. C gets back, he'll hold me responsible for any mess."

"I won't do anything like that. You can come with me and watch."

(Where the hell's Cardew? thought Max impatiently as he began moving around the room, noticing the absence of any figurines. Somehow, has he been tipped? Is he avoiding me? Was he watching the house when I came in? I had the feeling someone was watching me. I've had the feeling ever since I left Lois Corey's.)

"Mister?"

He moved his head and met the woman's eyes. "Yes?"

"You said you were from Missing Persons."

"That's right."

"Who's missing?"

"Tippy Blaney."

"Oh . . . I'm real sorry about that."

(So am I, sweetheart, so am I. But if he wasn't missing, I might never have known him.) Max pointed to a door. "That the bedroom?"

"Yes, it is." She moved past him to the door and opened it. Max went in. It was a small room furnished with twin beds. The wall was hung with more untalented Cardews. There was no sign of any figurines.

Max smiled at the woman. "Mr. Cardew doesn't go in much for bric-a-brac, does he? You know . . . little china figures, statuettes . . . things like that."

"Is that important?" she asked gravely.

"Yes. It's important."

She crossed to a sideboard, knelt and opened the bottom drawer. Max followed her and looked into the drawer. He stooped and with both hands scooped up two Dresden monkeys.

"See no evil . . . hear no evil . . ."

"And speak no evil. Beautiful, aren't they?"

It wasn't the woman who spoke.

Max turned to see what went with the voice.

He saw a handsome face marred by deep shadows under the eyes, red hair that grew to just below the nape of the neck, a brown tweed suit with frayed cuffs.

CHAPTER EIGHT

With an air of unconcerned disdain Edmund Cardew began removing his jacket as he led Max and the woman back into the living room. The detective was carrying the Dresden monkeys, which he carefully placed on a table.

"Emily," said Cardew with exaggerated patience, "I thought there was a rule about permitting people in here when I'm out."

Max spoke for her. "I'm Van Larsen of Missing Persons. It's about Tippy Blaney."

Cardew dropped his jacket on a chair and dismissed Emily with his eyes. She crossed to the door, picked up a shopping bag, opened the door, and over her shoulder directly to Max said, "Good night, Mr. Van Larsen. I hope the boy's safe." Without a word to Cardew she left.

The door latch and Max's voice snapped simultaneously. "Where's Tippy Blaney?"

Cardew was at the bar pouring himself a drink. "Want to sit at the table, touch fingers and try for him?"

Max sized him up swiftly and knew he could take him if it became necessary. Cardew made himself comfortable on the couch, crossed his right leg over the left and swung it lightly. Max remained standing by the table.

"When'd you steal these?" he asked, indicating the Dresden monkeys.

"They're Tippy's," said Cardew innocently. "He left them with me a couple of days ago."

"You work for Blaney," said Max. "I saw you there this afternoon."

"It's a living."

"So's stealing."

Cardew's voice continued to sustain innocence. "I don't steal. Tippy steals. I've tried to cover up for him. But he's the one who steals."

He managed to duck in time as a vase went sailing past his head and smashed against the door. But he didn't get to his feet in time as Max leaped at him, grabbed his left arm and twisted it ferociously behind his back, holding it tightly gripped with his right hand as his left tore Cardew's shirt sleeve to the elbow. Cardew's glass fell to the floor as he bit his lip in pain.

"How much a day?" hissed Max in his ear, slowly twisting the arm. "What's your bag? How much a day?"

"Let me up!" gasped Cardew.

"How much a day? How much a day?"

"Fifty!" cried Cardew. "Fifty! Jesus, Jesus, you're breaking it, you're breaking it!"

Max released his grip, moved away, and Cardew slumped back rubbing his arm.

"Now," said Max, breathing heavily, "who did the stealing? You . . . or my boy . . ."

(*Tippy* . . . not *my boy* . . . *Tippy.*)

"Your *boy*, as you so cozily call him, didn't exactly try to discourage me."

"The boy thought they were fakes . . . *worthless!*"

shouted Max. "Don't try to crap me! He thought they were fakes!"

"He knew better after Blaney fingered him! That didn't stop him from taking the monkeys!"

Max's hand shot forward and connected with Cardew's face. "You took those—and shall I tell you when? Within the past three days when you knew the kid was missing and it looked a cinch to pin it on him. He took the rap for you twice, you bastard, don't you even feel you *owe* him?"

I owe him. I know now I owe him. I know when it's time to pay a debt. Why don't you? Why doesn't everybody?

"I don't owe him," drawled Cardew. "I don't owe anybody. I need fifty bills a day and I don't care how I get it. The kid covered for me because I told him about the old man and the *paisanos*. The way he hates Blaney's guts he'd do anything to keep the son of a bitch's bowels ruptured." An almost coquettish look settled on his face. "You turning me in?"

"I might work you over first."

"Go ahead," the artist said, smiling. "I like it."

Max slapped him again and felt better. So did Cardew.

"Where's the kid?"

"I don't know."

"He had too much on you. You had to get rid of him. Blaney was wising up."

"Like hell."

"What about the secretary?"

"What secretary?"

"Blaney's."

"What about her?"

"She's on H too, isn't she?"

"How do I know!"

"Isn't she a friend of yours?"

"I had nothing to do with her," snapped Cardew.

"With so much in common?"

"I had nothing to do with her."

"When'd you last see the kid?"

"I don't remember."

"I'm not going to hit you again."

"Sadist."

Max hit him. "Better?"

"I saw him Sunday."

"When?"

"Late afternoon. Around six." The time element in Tippy's disappearance was narrowing. Max felt a bit better. "He wanted money. He thought I still had some figurines. I didn't. He tried to go through the place and I threw him out."

(Maybe he knows, Max hoped, maybe the boy told him.) "What was the money for?"

"I don't know."

"The truth."

"He wouldn't tell me, damn it . . . damn you . . . damn him!"

Max straightened up. "You slimy pig. You stinking slimy pig." He crossed to the phone and dialed the precinct, then both men sat in silence waiting for the squad car. Max glanced at his wristwatch. Sylvia Plotkin might be on her way to the Cloven Hoof.

"Did Tippy know you're on H?"

"Of course."

Max restrained his fingers from taking on a life of their own. "Why'd you let him hang around in this filth? Isn't there anything decent about you?"

"It doesn't bother Tippy. He likes it here." He watched Max rubbing his knuckles. "Well, he does. He's more welcome here than he is at home. Besides, we have something in common. We're fellow artists."

"Tippy," said Max pointedly, "is young enough to improve."

The color of Cardew's face now matched his hair, but he said nothing.

Max was looking around the room. "Where's your junk?"

"There isn't any. I'm out."

"Must I have the boys strip the place when they get here? Maybe take a knife and slash up your works of art?"

Cardew scratched his chin and then said through a yawn, "The desk . . . top drawer on the right."

"Stay glued," said Max to Cardew as he crossed to the desk. In the top drawer on the right he found a syringe, a spoon, and several packets of tissue paper containing heroin. He laid them out neatly and crossed back to Cardew.

"Who's your dealer?"

"The world's my dealer," smiled Cardew.

"Tippy ever see you take the stuff?"

"Never. Honest." It sounded sincere.

"I hope Blaney has a sense of humor."

"You're funnier."

"I hope you suffer hell."

"I'm beginning to. Let me take one last shot."

Max folded his arms and smiled.

The boy's agonized screams tore at Basil Kirby's ears.

"Oh, my God!" yelled Basil to the policemen. "Oh, my God! He's pinned under the wreckage!"

The policemen were making their way down the embankment when the gas tank exploded. Shielding their faces with their hands, they moved back, the wall of flames transposing the wreckage into a funeral pyre.

"Oh, my God!" cried Basil. "Oh, my God!" One of the policemen turned in time to see Basil's knees give way. He crumpled to the ground in a sobbing heap.

The armored truck was parked several hundred yards away from Cardew's brownstone on the opposite side of the street. The man behind the wheel flung *Playboy* aside and cursed under his breath when the squad car pulled up, and cursed again when the two policemen emerged, leading Edmund Cardew, with Max Van Larsen behind them. He felt better when only the policemen and Cardew got into the squad car and Van Larsen remained standing on the sidewalk watching two small boys play stoop ball. The man behind the wheel of the armored truck turned the key in the ignition, released the brake and let the motor purr as he waited for the detective to move.

In a café across the street from Cardew's brownstone, two biddies were perched on stools between the bar and the window, staring at the scene across the street starring Edmund Cardew. The clucking of their tongues invoked memories of Argentinita in *Three-Cornered Hat.* When the squad car pulled away, they continued transfixed by the detective watching two boys playing stoop ball. As though by mental telepathy, the detective turned and stared across the street at them.

(What the hell, Max thought, why not? I could use a shot of anything.) He started to cross the street to the café.

"Hey, mister!" piped a small-boy voice. "Get the ball!"

Max looked down and saw the ball rolling toward him. He stooped and picked it up. (Too hard for stoop ball, but times have changed since I was a boy. Everything in this rotten world's gotten harder. And where's that stupid son of a bitch behind the wheel of that armored truck heading?

Straight for me, for Christ's sake!)

He saw the truck bearing down on him and caught a glimpse of the face of the man behind the wheel. It was like a death's-head and it frightened him, but he raised his arm and hurled the ball before leaping to one side.

The man behind the wheel was startled to see the ball hurtling toward his windshield. *A face full of glass* . . . he panicked . . . *a face full of glass!* He twisted the wheel too quickly and the truck trembled as the back tires skidded and lost adhesion. He didn't see the detective pull his service revolver as he scrambled for safety, he only saw the sidewalk coming up at him, then the huge pane of glass that fronted the sleazy café and two biddies sitting open-mouthed and frozen on stools, too stunned with horror to move out of the path of the oncoming death wagon as it crashed through the store front and plowed into the screaming women, crashing them into the twisted wreckage of the bar and the bartender behind it.

There was no need to use the revolver. Max heard the biddies scream and the sickening sound of the crash and people shouting and feet running and a small boy crying and he hoped to God neither the women nor the murderer behind the wheel were dead.

He shoved the revolver back in the holster and raced toward the carnage. His and six other pairs of hands began pulling away the debris, and he heard a hysterical voice screaming, "Call an ambulance! For God's sake, call an ambulance!" and it wasn't until he looked back on the incident later that evening that he remembered the hysterical voice was his.

Sylvia Plotkin was at least half an hour too early for her date with Van Larsen, but she thought a long walk would help calm her nerves and settle her composure. She hummed "La Paloma" under her breath, turned a corner and segued into "La donna è mobile" and enjoyed the coolness of the tiny pearl hanging from the center of her turban and resting picturesquely on her forehead.

She devised and rejected a dozen variations of greetings for the detective. He'll speak first, she decided.

"*My, you look lovely*" or "*You're prompt, that's how I like my women, prompt*" or "*From the moment I set eyes on you this morning I knew I had to ask you out for dinner tonight*" and damn that ambulance siren for interrupting.

She smiled at the old lady sitting on an orange crate, who seemed to be smiling at her. The old lady wondered if the dizzy tart knew she had a run in her stocking.

The first ambulance carted away the women. The intern didn't hold out much hope for them. The second ambulance was for the bartender, who had fractured ribs, a broken arm, a broken leg, and an unbroken string of Irish oaths. The driver of the armored truck was unconscious, with a crushed rib cage, two broken arms (which pleased Van Larsen), and crushed kneecaps (which elated Van Larsen). He instructed the cop on the beat to accompany the murderous driver to the hospital, call Van Larsen at the precinct if and when the driver regained consciousness, and write down everything the driver said until Van Larsen got there. He watched the attendants lifting the driver into the ambulance.

I wish it was you, Marcus Blaney, I wish it was fat frog toad ugly you.

Marcus Blaney rubbed the palms of his hands with the Irish linen handkerchief, licked his lips nervously, and stared with frustration and anger at the private telephone. Mercifully, it rang.

"What took you so long?" he shouted into the mouthpiece.

"Who the *hell* do you think this is?" It was Wilma. "What the *hell* are you still doing in the office? I'm *starving!*"

"So starve. Now get off. I'm expecting an important call."

"Don't *hang up!*" she screeched.

The bitch reads minds. He pulled the phone back to his ear.

"He's seen Lois!"

"Van Larsen?"

"Well, who else would I mean? He knows she's *Laura!* He knows *everything!*" She paused, but Blaney said nothing, so she continued. "Does it mean *trouble?*"

"I don't know yet."

"You're too calm."

"The *paisanos* are getting to him."

"Oh." He welcomed what he interpreted as relief in her voice. Sadly Wilma was mentally waving goodbye to any hopes of a toss in the hay with Van Larsen.

"That's the call I'm waiting for," said Marcus.

"I hope he frightens easy," she said weakly.

"Maybe."

"Call me back when you know."

"I'll come straight home."

"Call me *first.*"

"Drop dead."

He hung up and wiped the sweat from the phone. He wished he had a clean handkerchief with which to wipe the sweat from his brow. He wished he had a clean handkerchief with which to wipe his slate clean. He wished a lot of wishes he knew would never be granted, and then cursed the day he fell in love with a broad named Wilma Cecci and married her and took her sister's bastard into his home.

A squad car delivered Max to his precinct in five minutes flat.

In his office, he dialed Sylvia Plotkin to tell her he'd be late and got her answering service after nine rings. He hung up without leaving a message. Then he crossed to the mirror and decided he didn't look too bad, all things considered. There was a lot to do but no time in which to do it if he didn't want Sylvia Plotkin cooling her heels at the Cloven Hoof. His report might just as well wait until after he saw Bibi Something. He could come back later and file it then.

If Bibi Something offered no lead, there might be a need to retrace his steps or briefly veer off on another tangent named Antonia Burgess. His intuition about her had been pecking away at him on and off from their meeting in the office.

He crossed back to the desk, sat down, and lit a cigarette. The day's progression, from the Blaneys' reporting Tippy missing to the armored truck bearing down on him, was like one of those inventions Rube Goldberg used to dream up in the comic strips. Somewhere in the maze there had to be the answer to why Tippy Blaney disappeared. Someone in today's parade of cockeyed creatures was playing him for a sucker.

He groaned inwardly and the cigarette tasted bitter.

(When I find the kid, I wonder if he'll like me. I'd like him to like me. I want to be his friend, his companion, his mentor. It's not too late to help set the boy right. It's not too late to apply balm to the bruises and the wounds. He's only seventeen and it's not too late. I'll help him accept his situation, accept Lois Corey as his mother, accept the past as an unavoidable dirty trick fate frequently played on innocent kids, like the dirty trick fate played on a boy named Derek Nils Van Larsen by giving him me for a father.)

Max wept.

Five minutes later he ordered a tracer on Marcus Mario Laggio Blaney. He wasn't too surprised to be told immediately that Blaney's operation had been under surveillance for several months. They weren't too surprised to hear an attempt had been made on Max's life. Everybody felt they were getting some place and worth their salaries and more.

Max glanced at his wristwatch and hoped Sylvia Plotkin wasn't thinking she'd been stood up. Then his phone rang and Herb Roper in Homicide asked him if he could spare a minute. He couldn't but he said he could.

Herb Roper was one of the few associates Max tolerated. He had read and enjoyed *The Tin Drum* and had seen *Marat/Sade* twice. Max told him he had a date waiting, and Roper dismissed the statement by pointing to a chair.

"Got myself a fresh murder victim," said Roper like a man who had traded his automobile for a new model. Max was patient, knowing Roper as a detective who relished preliminaries, a man who went to the movies and voiced disappointment if he missed the credits. "It overlaps the Blaney kid's disappearance."

Max sat up tensely.

"Found a broad with her neck broken in the front seat of her car in a parking lot on West Broadway near the

Blaney warehouse. Turns out she worked for Blaney. Antonia Burgess. His secretary. Her arms looked like pincushions without pins."

Max filled in Roper on Edmund Cardew and then both men sat back and stared at each other.

"The plot sickens," said Roper. "A kid disappears, his father's secretary is murdered, and we haul in a junkie who works for old dad."

"Have you contacted Blaney?"

"Been dialing his house for an hour and all I get is a busy signal."

"Try his office. He may be working late."

"Check. If that doesn't get a result, I'll send squad cars to both places, house and office. Well," sighed Roper, "you keep after the kid. Maybe if you find him we can fit the square pegs into the square holes. I'll have a chat with friend Cardew in the meantime. Between us we ought to be able to come up with some answers. Don't keep your date waiting."

"It's the kid's teacher."

"Shame on you."

"Nice lady. We're meeting at a place where the boy's girl friend works. You may as well know it, she's my last lead."

Roper smiled. "Sometimes one thing leads to another. Keep in touch."

"Will do."

"By the way," said Roper as Max was halfway out of his office, "have you read any of Jakov Lind's stuff? Delicious!"

CHAPTER NINE

Sylvia Plotkin liked Bleecker Street. She didn't care how often it was exposed by the *New York Post,* it was a hell of a lot more fun and a hell of a lot more interesting and a hell of a lot more colorful than the Grand Concourse. She had circled the block five times, and now that her wristwatch told her it was five past nine, she decided it was time to enter the Cloven Hoof.

Standing in the doorway, she could see it was jammed. The bar was at least fifty deep with an assortment of Village types and tourists. All the dozen or so tables were occupied. The waitresses were dressed in red leotards, red blouses, and red hoods with two tiny horns. When one waitress turned around, she saw a black tail hanging limply from the girl's rear end. At the farthest end of the room, on a raised platform, three boys in Buster Brown haircuts, with khaki shirts unbuttoned to their midriffs, exposing various degrees of bare, hairy or sunken chest, were desultorily plucking guitars and wondering where all the flowers had gone.

Sylvia stood glued to the doorway, hoping somewhere in the crush ahead of her, Detective Max (I hope you like homemade chicken soup) Van Larsen would see her and claim her.

Satan appeared. He was encased in red from head to toe, two horns on the head, a pitchfork in his left hand, and a black velvet cape around his shoulders. Most of his angular face was covered with a matted beard, and when he spoke to her, Sylvia was grateful Satan lithped.

"Greetingth, thithter!" Sylvia was also grateful he was a mezzo-soprano. Ever since Gladys Swarthout she favored mezzo-sopranos. "Abandon hope all ye who enter here!"

Sylvia smiled congenially. "I'm expecting to meet somebody."

"Who ithn't?"

"His name is Van Larsen."

"Tho?" He was resting on the pitchfork, prong side down.

"Doesn't he have a reservation?"

"Thith ith hell, thweetie, not the Platha."

"Oh. Well, I don't see him anywhere. Is there somewhere I can wait?"

"You could try a thqueeth at the bar."

She wondered if she ought to ask for Bibi Something. The din in the room was near-deafening and the trio in the rear seemed oblivious to it as they segued into "What Now, My Love."

"Do you have a waitress here named Bibi?"

"What about her?"

Sylvia renewed her open-school-week smile usually reserved for parents, the one with the cleverly concealed message: Go drop dead. "She's a friend of one of my students."

(Thweet Jethuth, thought Satan, a vigilante.) "We

don't permit youngthterth under eighteen in here unleth accompanied by an adult."

Sylvia had counted at least ten youngthterth at the bar, but live and let live. She decided to treat Satan the way she would her student Rodriguez. "Listen, smart ass, none of your lip. Do you have Bibi here or don't you have a Bibi here and don't you know how to talk to a lady?"

"Thorry," he sniffed. "Bibi'th thome plathe in the back and very buthy at the moment."

Sylvia felt the hand on her shoulder and didn't have to turn around immediately to look at the body it belonged to. She had fantasied for hours what the touch would feel like, and she wasn't disappointed. It was gentle though firm, affectionate though restrained, protective though light. She turned around.

"Oh, thank God."

"Sorry I'm late," said Van Larsen.

Miraculously, Satan produced a table for them in the rear of the club near the trio. Max ordered a Scotch for himself and a vodka sour (no sugar) for Sylvia, who beamed at him as she removed her black gloves with the imitation Belgian lace trimming (Korvette's, but in this lighting they could be Saks). Satan promised to send Bibi Something to them eventually and went to place their order at the bar.

"Well, here we are!" trilled Sylvia.

"Thought I'd never make it. I phoned you over half an hour ago"—her heart sank—"to tell you I'd be late"—

her heart bounced back—"and ran like a bastard to get here."

Thirty minutes and another round of drinks later Max filled her in on his day, from Madame Vilna to the tragic Prince of Darkness to Laura Cecci and the story of Tippy's origins, through which Sylvia Plotkin alternately oh no!'d and poor darling'd (meaning Tippy, not Max), through to the armored truck and his narrow escape from death, through which Sylvia Plotkin alternately oh no!'d and poor darling'd (meaning Max, not Tippy).

"Well," exhaled Sylvia when Max paused, "you've certainly had a day!"

Max signaled for a third round of drinks, inwardly grateful for no *Goodness, no more for me two's my limit* from round, shining, warm and deeply interested hang-on-every-word-like-a-good-listener-ought-to Sylvia Plotkin.

"There's more."

Sylvia leaned forward eagerly and listened with horror to the facts about Antonia Burgess' murder. When he was finished, she grasped her third vodka sour (no sugar) and exclaimed, "Good God! You're a Sunday supplement. What happens next?"

"Next," said Max, "I try to talk to Bibi Something, if it's possible in this musical boiler factory" (the trio had long since given way to a Negro jazz quartet that laid heavy emphasis on the soprano saxophone) "and get something to eat, and not necessarily here if you'd rather not."

"Frankly," said Sylvia, "I passed a delicatessen a couple of doors back that smelled very inviting."

"You're on. Let's try and land Bibi."

On cue, a waitress came to the table and said, "You want to see me? I'm Bibi."

Max liked her pixie-face. "I'm Max Van Larsen. Detective Van Larsen."

Her mouth formed an O but no sound emerged.

"It's about Tippy. You know he's missing?"

She nodded.

"Look," said Max, "it's impossible to talk here. Can you get away for a few minutes?"

"I can try."

He liked her voice. It was smooth, easy and pleasant. "It's important. Let me fix it with your boss."

"That's not necessary," she said. "Just name the place. I'll join you there."

"You know the delicatessen down the street?"

She nodded. "Ginsberg's Ghetto. I'll tell your waitress to bring the check."

"Why can't you tell *me* what it's in reference to?" Wilma yapped peevishly into the mouthpiece. Her grip on the phone was tighter than her grip on herself. "If this is in reference to my son, after all, I'm his *mother*."

(Lady, thought Roper, your school of acting died with Helen Twelvetrees.)

"This has nothing to do with your son," said Roper with overemphasized patience. "Have you any idea where your husband can be reached?"

(Oh, the hell with it, decided Wilma.) "You might try his office!" her barbed exclamation point stinging Roper's eardrum. "He said he'd be working late tonight." She slammed the phone down.

Roper said "Thank you" to the dial tone.

Wilma sat with her arms tightly folded and tapping a foot angrily. Now what? What's the fresh can of peas? She sifted a variety of thoughts in search of a possible answer. (Maybe more stuff's been stolen. Stuff he hasn't told me about. He promised not to call the cops in again the next time the kid took anything. But Marcus' promises are like the Long Island Rail Road. Unreliable. Oh, the hell with it. The hell with Tippy. Screw Marcus. Up Marcus.)

She crossed to the television set and turned up the sound. With panther-like strides she walked to the easy chair and settled into it with one foot tucked under. (Detective Roper, she fumed to herself, you are rude, officious and a fink. You are a blood brother to Detective Van Larsen.) She stared at the television screen. *Damn.* She'd missed the best scene.The voice from the set commanded Wilma's undivided attention.

"And *what,*" said Bette Davis in a tremulous voice, "is prognosis *negative?*"

Marcus Blaney held the private phone to his ear, perspiring, blinking his eyes agitatedly, rolling the Irish linen handkerchief into a tight little ball and kneading it. His frog eyes strained and popped as he croaked an occasional "Now listen!" and "Wait a minute!" into the mouthpiece, spraying it with spittle from the nervous pools that formed and gurgled in his mouth. The other end of the line was impervious to his weak attempts at excuses and suggestions, at the pallid imprecations lobbed at a bungling armored truck driver who lay dying in a nearby hospital.

By the solitary lamplight in his office, Marcus looked older and uglier. As though by the magic of movie trickery he could feel his skin mottle and shrivel and he thought he would crumble and disappear in a puff of dust. It might be preferable to the fate promised him by the voice on the other end.

The desk phone rang and Marcus scowled at it. There was no point in answering. At this hour it could only be a wrong number.

There was a pause in the tirade at the other end of the private wire brought on by a hacking cough, and Marcus seized the opportunity and leaped into the breach. "If the bastard croaks, we're okay then! The cops can't trace the truck! Can't somebody get to Cardew . . . ?"

The other end recovered rapidly. The stream of invective that poured out of the receiver inundated and near-drowned the frog. He ran the ball of handkerchief across his forehead. He renewed attempts of "Now listen!" and "Wait a minute!" but knew that listening and time were running out.

Five minutes later the overworked phone rested in its cradle and the frog sat slumped in his seat, staring at the floor, pummeling his brain to provide a solution, an out, rescue, salvation. Tippy. Bastard. Lois. Laura. Wilma. Figurines. Cardew. *Paisanos*. Beatings. Antonia. Murder. Tippy. Wilma.

(I'll kill her.

"It's my sister's baby. My own flesh and blood. I can't let her give it away! It would be a sin! Ah, look at the cute little thing. Come on, Mario, let's take the kid. It's such an itty-bitty little thing. How much could it eat?"

It could eat a lot. It could eat up my whole life. What do I do now? Who's to turn to? My devoted wife?

My devoted wife.)

He rushed for the door.

Through the unwashed bus window Basil Kirby read the sign LINCOLN TUNNEL, FIVE MILES.

(Don't rush, Mr. Bus Driver. Ease up on the pedal. I need more time to pull myself together. I've just been through hell and that's not like going through Youngstown, Ohio. I watched a kid go up in flames today and I don't think I'll ever get the stench out of my nostrils. I watched a boy die, and all it made me think is, Life is cheap. That's not what I should be thinking. Life is dear and precious and I want as much of it as I can get. I need Lois. Lois needs me. Will she understand when I explain it all to her? When will my hands stop trembling?)

I will be calm. I will be serene. I shall find peace.

Tears trickled down Wilma Blaney's cheeks, her damp handkerchief having lost its effectiveness two reels and eight commercials back.

(Don't let her die, pleaded Wilma silently, don't let her die. At least ten times I've seen this picture and every time she dies. Just once . . . just once . . . by some miracle, let her live to enjoy this beautiful house in Maine and her crocuses and the love of her German shepherds and the gentle tickle of George Brent's mustache when he kisses her.

"Oh!" said Bette Davis as she planted another bulb in her garden. "There's going to be a storm!"

Geraldine Fitzgerald looked at the sky. There was a very bright sun and not a sign of a cloud. It was the kind of perfect weather specialized in by the Brothers Warner. Geraldine stared at Bette and her hand flew to her mouth in horror. Bette's hand was stretched out in front of her.

"But I can feel the sun on my hand," said Bette tenderly, bravely.

A sob escaped from Geraldine's throat and from Wilma's throat. Not only Bette—I love you, Bette!—but Max Steiner's syrupy music was hacking at her sympathy.)

She didn't hear the door open or Marcus' stealthy tread across the thickly carpeted floor. She knew he was there when she felt the sharp sting of the blow he dealt her face with his pudgy palm. She cringed in the chair and covered her face with her hands as blow after blow rained down on her, screaming, crying, then groping blindly for something with which to strike back, completely oblivious of Bette's quiet, peaceful, and welcome death in the solitude and darkness of her beautifully furnished Warner Brothers bedroom.

"Sign the petition!" bellowed the fat girl in the fluffy blouse and blue jeans seated at the bridge table on the curb outside the Bleecker Street delicatessen. "Help end police harassment in Greenwich Village! Support Kenneth Anger and 'Scorpio Rising'!"

Max guided Sylvia Plotkin into the delicatessen, and

an eager headwaiter bowed them to a table near the window.

"We're expecting someone else," Max told the headwaiter, increasing his eagerness because the establishment was sparsely occupied and had been sparsely occupied since the newspapers began warning tourists away from the area.

"I wanna open the movie with a shot of Auschwitz," giggled the malevolent male voice a few tables away, "and we dolly in on the entrance over which is a sign 'All Baking Done on Premises.' Mad mad mad, baby! Jonas Mekas'll love it!"

Sylvia Plotkin winced inwardly, then folded her arms on the table and studied the detective's tired face as he lit a cigarette. "You smoke too much," she wanted to tell him, but she didn't know him well enough (yet) and checked herself. "You're very tired, aren't you?"

He nodded as he exhaled a perfect smoke ring. Sylvia envisioned it as the setting for a two-carat diamond.

"Hungry?" he asked her.

"I can wait. Can we get some coffee?"

Max ordered two coffees.

"Do you always work this hard when you're on a case?" (Who do you go home to at night? Who sits alone and worries for your safety and well-being? Who listens with interest and with love when you gobble a late supper and between mouthfuls relate the fascinating facts of the day's activities?)

"I live alone," said Max, as though reading her mind. "My time's my own. I've got nothing but time."

Sylvia's eyes dropped to the black armband, then back to his face. "Did you lose your wife?"

"Yes," said Max, "and my boy."

"How terrible." Sylvia ached for him.

"Yes."

The waiter brought their coffees and they sat in silence until he left.

Max toyed with a teaspoon. "It was an automobile crash. Week before last."

"Oh, how awful." There was almost no strength in her whisper.

Max looked at her steadily. "We didn't get along. We never did."

"Oh." (Did you wish her dead? Are you that kind of a man? Does a nice person like you wish people dead? Are appearances deceiving?)

"I wasn't much of a father either." (Be patient, Sylvia Plotkin, and hear me out. Be patient and try to understand. I haven't realized until today how badly I need someone to talk to.) "Maybe that's why this missing boy's gotten under my skin."

"I understand that."

"I took a week off after the funeral. I didn't want to, but I did. I come back and look what I get handed. The case of a missing boy who's been no better off than my own son."

"That's life."

She blew on her coffee and sipped. Max tapped some ash into a tray and picked a piece of tobacco from his lower lip.

"I should never have married her."

Sylvia sloshed some coffee into her saucer and placed a paper napkin under the cup. "Same with me and Isaac," she said. "My ex . . . Isaac. We grew up together. To a certain point, that is. He's remarried now. A beautician, I'm told." She managed a smile but she knew it didn't look right.

"My wife and I had nothing in common," said Max, "except the boy." (Don't pass judgment yet, Sylvia Plotkin. Just listen in what little time we have until Bibi Something gets here and sets me back on that other track. Just listen. I'm listening with you. I'm trying to release a hang-up that's been tied in a little knot at the bottom of my gorge for thirteen years, maybe longer. It has to surface sooner or later. It must. I want to be rid of it.) "I was a patrolman when I met her and we had an affair. I only married her because she was pregnant."

Sylvia blinked her eyes as she struggled for words but they remained elusive. She nodded. (You married beneath you.)

"There was just nothing to talk about. You see . . . I like good music . . ."

(So do I.)

". . . and stimulating books . . ."

(Ditto.)

". . . and art galleries and museums . . ."

(You're a living doll.)

". . . and there was never a way of sharing it with her."

(Did you try?)

"I come from what they call very solid Dutch stock." He was grinning and she was glad his teeth were in excellent shape. "My father was sort of a martinet. I never knew my mother. She died when I was three. We lived on this farm in upstate New York outside Oneonta."

(I spent two weeks at a lovely resort near there four summers ago but all they could offer me was a shoe salesman and a C.P.A with acne. I'll tell him about that some other time.)

"After the war I stayed in New York. I hadn't been trained for anything special, so I drifted into the police force. I guess it was in my blood all the time and I never realized it. Maybe hereditary." He took a sip of coffee.

"What was your boy like?" asked Sylvia.

Max remarried the cup to the saucer and stubbed out his cigarette. "I'm ashamed to say I don't really know. He never saw very much of me. I guess I frightened him." (*Martinet?*) Max shrugged weakly. "They were just two intruders in my life . . . the boy and his mother. I guess I should have cut out on them years ago. But I couldn't do it. Maybe if I had, they'd still be alive today."

(What does he mean by that? wondered Sylvia).

"I had the whole thing rationalized until this Tippy thing came up this morning. Here's a kid I never met in my life and I know more about him in twelve hours than I knew about my own son in thirteen years."

He was lighting another cigarette and having trouble keeping his hand steady.

"It's crazy maybe, but I want to find that boy . . . Tippy . . . and know him better. Hasn't something like that ever happened to you?"

(Are you *blind?* What do you think I'm doing here?)

"It certainly has," she said a bit too airily. "Two days after I shed my Isaac and got back from Mexico. Seriously . . . I'm glad you feel this way about Tippy. And you shouldn't eat yourself up so much about your wife and son. After all, it isn't as though what happened to them, tragic as it is, was your fault."

"But it was," said Max.

Sylvia waited.

"She left a note. I found it that night after I identified the bodies. I burned the note. I was too ashamed. She destroyed herself and the boy. Would you like some more coffee?"

CHAPTER TEN

"He must be some kind of a nut or something," the perplexed detective was telling Roper. "Every time we ask him a question he says, 'Go ahead . . . hit me.' "

"Don't lay a finger on him."

"He begged me for a shot of H."

"That's good," said Porter, "then we'll get what we want out of him in time. Did you take my copy of *Games People Play*?"

A neighbor heard Wilma screaming, and called the police, but when the squad car arrived, the Blaneys were gone.

"I was at my window when I saw her come running out of the house," explained the neighbor to the uniformed men, having introduced herself as Elsie Lee Mackintosh, a librarian. "She was crying something terrible. She got into her car and drove away and almost hit some kids playing stick ball in the street. Then *he* came out of the house and it was *awful*. There was blood on the left side of his head, and he was holding this handkerchief to the wound, I guess, and he tried to hail a cab but at least three passed him by because you can imagine what they must have thought seeing a bleeding man, then finally one stopped for him and he got in and they drove off in the direction she'd gone because I suppose he figured where she was going . . . and I swear to God, New York is a jungle, an absolute *jungle.*"

Bibi Something entered the delicatessen. She had changed into a sack dress, which almost obscured the fine line of her body, which, back at the Cloven Hoof, Max had silently admired and Sylvia had carefully studied. Bibi had seen them through the window and gone directly to their table. Sylvia made room for her on her side of the booth and Bibi sat down and folded her hands on the table.

"Would you like something?" Max asked her.

"No, thanks," she said in a pleasant, well-modulated voice. "I don't have much time. It's my last night at the place but I like to play fair."

"You found a better job?" asked Sylvia for openers.

"I'm going home," replied Bibi. "I've had New York."

(And vice versa? wondered Max.)

"I've been here two years and it's all been a big nothing. So I'm going home. Chicago. No better, but no worse. My mother's glad. I've got three brothers and two sisters and she needs help." She began constructing a pyramid of sugar cubes. "I guess I'll miss Tippy. I phoned his house the other day to tell him I was going home. That's when I found out he'd gone away."

"When was the last time you saw him?" asked Max.

"Sunday morning. He spent Saturday night with me." Sylvia admired her directness. "I guess I should have realized then he had no intention of ever going home again."

"Why?"

"Well . . ." She razed the pyramid. "He'd had this awful row with his father Friday morning. I suppose you know they don't get along. He's beat up Tippy before."

Sylvia saw Max's hand form a fist.

Bibi moistened her lips and continued. "Tippy had some crazy idea about him and me going away together."

(Five hundred dollars.)

"But that was crazy," continued Bibi. "I'm five years older than he is, but I guess in his way, he's ten years older than me. He knows so much about so much for seventeen."

(Do I detect pain in your eyes? wondered Max.)

"But it wouldn't have been any good," sighed Bibi, "and I knew it, and I guess deep down he knew it too."

"He tried to get five hundred dollars from his father," said Max. "Was it to go away with?"

"Well, no . . ." She spoke hesitantly. "I think that was for something else, but don't ask me what because I can't tell you."

Max decided not to press her for the moment.

"When he left me Sunday morning, it was to go see his Aunt Lois. He didn't think she had any money, but he thought he'd give it a try. He'd been asking everyone he knew. No one would help him. Isn't it funny how rotten people you thought were your friends can turn out to be?"

(I'm listening between the lines, thought Max. I know that statement is based on experience.)

Sylvia was patting Bibi's hand. "Dear," began Sylvia

in her best board-of-education voice, "this is apropos of nothing, but what in heaven is your last name?"

Bibi smiled. "Are you ready? Dumas. No relation I'm sure, but Tippy thinks it's a hoot. My family's French-Canadian originally."

"How long have you known Tippy?" asked Max.

"Couple of months." She leaned back and smiled. "We met at a sit-in. Down with war. But I guess nobody paid us much attention."

Sylvia shook her head sadly and sipped her cold coffee.

Max leaned forward. "How much did Tippy tell you about himself?"

"Like what?" Her voice was guarded.

"I think you know what I'm talking about."

"Well . . . you're a detective." She whispered *detective* as though it were sacred. "I suppose you've already found out most of it. I guess it comes as a shock to find out your parents aren't really your parents, although" —she laughed musically—"I really think it made Tippy very happy because he can't stand the Blaneys. Not even her really, though she doesn't treat him too badly. He prefers his Aunt Lois. I think he found out something about her too, but he wouldn't tell me what it was. He knew a lot of things about Blaney too, and I think even some things even Blaney didn't know, but I'm just guessing at that. He wrote a funny poem about Blaney."

Max exchanged a glance with Sylvia.

"When was this?" he asked Bibi.

"Saturday night at my place."

"What did he do with it?"

"He said he was going to send it to that magazine."

She began snapping her fingers as a prod for her faulty memory.

"*Sappho?*"

"That's it," she said. "But first he said he was going to read it to Blaney 'and watch the fat slob sweat.' "

Max paled. "Do you know if he did?"

"I'm sorry. I haven't seen or heard from Tippy since Sunday morning. That's the truth."

Max stared out the window at the fat girl and her petitions and the multitudes ignoring her and thought of Marcus the Frog, who thought he might have seen Tippy at a rally in Washington Square yesterday. Or had he smoothly altered the time, the place, the day? Sylvia's voice cut into his thoughts. She was directing a question at Bibi.

"I suppose this is none of my business, dear, but are you in love with Tippy?"

Max turned in time to see Bibi purse her lips quixotically. "No, not the way you should be when you say you're in love. That's why I'm going home. Tippy and me, we've got nowhere to go from here. He doesn't think so, but I know better. In some things I'm smarter." She looked at Max. "I better be getting back. Is there anything else?"

Max shook his head. "I appreciate your help."

"I hope he's okay. Would you let me know? I'm not leaving until Saturday." She gave Max her address, a rooming house on Greenwich Avenue, and he dutifully penciled it onto one of his sheets of paper. Then Bibi shook hands with both of them and left.

"Poor kid," commented Sylvia.

Max wasn't listening.

"Hey!"

He looked up.

"Where are you?"

"I've got to get to Marcus Blaney. Excuse me a minute. I want to call the precinct." He arose and crossed to the phone booth indicated to him by the headwaiter.

Sylvia stared into the empty coffee cup. (I'm a very educated lady. I hold a license to teach school in New York City. I've been married and learned even more from that. I've met a man named Max Van Larsen and my knowledge increases. I've been listening to and studying a girl named Bibi Dumas who seems wise beyond her years and, like Tippy, who is too soon a man, she is too soon a woman. I think I have even learned something that I think has eluded my Max Van Larsen, and when he comes back to the table, I guess I'd better tell him. It's too early in our relationship to start keeping things from him.)

The Prince of Darkness sat on the floor of the loft of the derelict building, his cheek resting against a window sill, staring past jagged pieces of broken glass at the festivities in the street below. The building shook again as it had been shaking from time to time during the past two hours when he heard feet running across the roof. He saw a policeman in the street gesturing threateningly toward the roof, shouting a warning to the kids up there to get off, but Ashley knew the kids couldn't hear him. He couldn't hear the policeman, how could they? Plaster silt trickled down from the cracked ceiling, adding jagged dirty white stripes to his black cloak, powdering his tear-streaked face and clogging his mouth and nostrils, but it didn't matter. Nothing mattered any longer except to be with Tippy. His lips formed the name and he wept again.

Clifton Southford studied his reflection in the floor-length mirror in his bedroom. He was dressed in a pink and yellow toga that came to his knees. On his head perched a laurel wreath of his own design, gold and silver leaves, cut, painted, and polished by himself and welded to an iron halo. His feet were shod in golden sandals with silver laces that tied midway up his calves. Attached to his wrist was a stuffed white dove with outspread wings that could be used as a fan if the evening became humid. In his left hand he held a four-foot-long staff that ended in a crook which might have been handed down from generation to generation beginning with Bo-Peep. Across the back of the tunic he had carefully sewn PAX. He hoped the morons at the block party would understand *pax* was Latin for *peace*. He stepped back a few feet for a better perspective and resisted an urge to fling himself at the mirror and cover his image with kisses.

"I love you, Clifton Southford, Esquire!" he shouted gleefully at the mirror. "I love you love you love you!"

Across his eyes he placed a domino mask that attached at the ears. He thought he looked deliciously mysterious. He looked the way he knew he would have looked had he been born in an era when he would have sought and won the favors of an Emperor Hadrian.

"But it's never too late!" he mused aloud cheerfully. "There are still favors to be won, and little nymphs to bestow them!" He reassured himself that the crisp five-dollar bills were safely stashed in the toga's hidden pocket. Sometimes little nymphs can drive a very hard bargain.

◆

Madame Vilna emerged from the building on West Broadway that housed the Workmen's Circle meeting room, her beautiful head held high with pride. The reading had gone beautifully. Even the idiot amateur she had recruited at the last minute to assist her had done surprisingly well. He was no Tippeleh, but he passed muster. His reading of Tippeleh's poems wasn't as impassioned as Tippeleh's would have been, but the audience of elderly men and women applauded as though the shade of T. S. Eliot had declaimed before them. A surprisingly triumphant evening, mused the elated Madame Vilna. Now to gather new laurels. On to the peace rally. On to the block party where a hush would fall over the revelers when she mounted the platform and recited what must surely be Tippeleh's most inspired poetry to date. If only he were there to read with her. If only so many things . . . She hailed a taxi.

◆

Wilma left her car in a parking lot three blocks from Lois'. She'd driven past the street and seen the crush and heard the girl folk singer over the loud speaker nasalizing about the *fallen* and the *lost* and the *shrouded youth,* which ingeniously managed to rhyme with *crowded truth,* and heard firecrackers and police whistles, and in the moment she cursed them all for making the street impassable, was struck by the realization that it was a stroke of good luck. Lois' would be the first place Marcus would think of looking for her. Where was there to flee to other than out of the city? She'd call Lois, tell her where she was parked, tell her where to direct Van Larsen to find her when he picked up the message she had left for him at the precinct. After cruising around for five minutes, finding the parking lot, repairing her smarting face in the rear-view mirror, she had time to review her decision. No regrets. Goodbye, Marcus Mario. "I hate to see you go, I hate to see you go," she sang to herself. "I hope to hell you never come back, I hate to see you go."

"My brother-in-law's a doctor, mister," said the cab driver to Marcus' reflection in his rear-view mirror. "He lives over on Tenth. You ought to let him look at that cut."

"It stopped bleeding," said Marcus sharply.

"Yeah, but you got blood all over you, mister. Don't you want to stop some place and clean up? There's a bar over near Bank with a back entrance right near the john. You know, supposing some cop sees you . . ."

Marcus told him to drive to the bar.

Edmund Cardew flung himself against the wall of his cell and beat his fists against the cement until they were raw and bleeding. His body was racked with pain, his skin clammy with perspiration, his mouth desert-dry with thirst, and his brain was hammering at his skull begging for release.

(Why didn't I give myself the shot before I went home? Why'd I wait? Why was I so cocksure? I've got to fight the delirium. I've got to fight it. You don't know half the things you're saying when you're delirious. I might blow the whole gaff and I've got the frigging fuzz running around in circles. I've got to keep them in orbit.)

The guard watching Edmund Cardew through the tiny window in the door smiled. He liked watching the hopheads in the withdrawal period. He did imitations of them on Saturday nights when he and the wife had the neighbors in. The neighbors loved his beer and his cold cuts and his imitations. He loved doing his imitations. He loved watching the hopheads. They all did the same thing. Hit the walls. Tore at their hair. Cried to God, who was usually busy elsewhere. Sometimes they hurt themselves seriously. You'd think they'd never forget the pain, the agony, the horror of it. But most of them were forgetful. Most of them were brought in again sooner or later. And he'd watch them and do his imitations and watch them and do his imitations and he was positive the rut he was in was a better rut than anybody else's.

The phone rang and Lois Corey left her seat at the window to answer it. She had an excellent view of the speaker's platform and the entertainment was proving to be much better than she had expected, not that anyone was giving it much attention. They were too busy pushing and jostling and laughing and screaming and feeling each other up and tearing masks from each other's faces and letting out whoops of recognitions and the cops were forever chasing the kids off the roofs, especially off the roof of the rotting old derelict next door because it wasn't safe and should have been torn down months ago.

(Maybe it's Van Larsen. Maybe they've found Tippy. Maybe.)

"Hello?"

It was Wilma. "Are you alone?"

"Yes."

"Listen carefully. Mario's in trouble." Not *Marcus*? It must be very serious trouble. "It's all because of Tippy and those figurines, and don't give me any arguments, there's no time! He beat me up tonight." Lois felt her temples throbbing. "He'd of killed me if I hadn't clipped him on the head with the heel of my shoe. He's probably out looking for me. He may be coming to your place." (To beat me up too? wondered Lois.) "Whatever he asks, you haven't heard from me, you hear?"

Silence.

"*Lois!*"

"Yes, yes, I'm listening." (Oh, come home to me, Basil!)

"I left a message for Van Larsen at his precinct. I left your number. I got to see him as soon as you hear from him. I'm going to tell you where I'm parked, but on Mama's grave you got to promise not to tell Marcus! *Promise!*"

"I promise." She listened to Wilma's instructions carefully and memorized them.

"I'm going to sit in a coffee house across the street from the car and watch for Van Larsen. Tell him that, but dear God, don't tell Marcus. He won't lay a finger on you. I know he won't. Oh God, Lois, pray for me."

"I will," said Lois, her fingers touching the Christian Science Reader. "I'll pray for all of us. Especially Tippy."

She hung up. (Scandal again. Maybe worse than even before. I'll lose Basil positively. There's nothing left.)

She picked up the Reader, turned to her favorite passage, and read.

Sylvia Plotkin hated coping with more than one hunger at a time. She needed food, she needed love, and she needed to be needed. She watched Van Larsen make first one phone call, a long one, then another and then another, and began to miss him terribly. He was just across the restaurant in a phone booth, but it could just as well have been Africa.

(I can't be in love with him, thought Sylvia, because it's much too soon. Besides, all I am to him so far is a sounding board. That terrible revelation about his wife and child. How easily he told it—or was it because he was telling it to me? And the way he feels about Tippy. I like that. I understand that. Feeling for somebody is home territory. Since Isaac, I haven't really felt for anybody except once Paul Newman. Oh, now and then one of the kids reach me, like Tippy, but that's not the same thing.

I hope this date with Max isn't a one-shot. Did he ask me out because he needed somebody to talk to, or does he like me for myself? What did I do when we met this morning that was so special? If I knew, I could work on it and refine it and raise it to the level of a fine art and use it again and again in case Max Van Larsen forgets my phone number after tonight. But I'm in the book. Plotkin, Sylvia. Please like me, Max Van Larsen. I'll even settle for your occasional company. Friends. No strings. Right now I'll settle for anything.)

Max was back sitting opposite her.

"Sorry to be so long. I checked in at the precinct. There's been trouble at the Blaneys'. They've both disappeared."

Sylvia's eyebrows flew up.

Max was lighting a cigarette.

(You smoke too much. Think of those precious lungs!)

Max exhaled and continued. "Apparently Wilma Blaney tried to reach me half an hour ago. She left Lois Corey's number."

"Did you try it?"

"Several times. Damn line's busy. I'll try again in a few minutes. Holy investigation!" He slapped his forehead with the palm of his hand. "You must be starving!"

(For a lot of things, darling man.)

"I was wondering when you'd ask," said Sylvia sweetly.

"We'll have to grab something in a hurry."

They ordered pastramis on rye and coffee, and Max chain-smoked his way to the next cigarette.

"Mr. Detective," said Sylvia, "I've been doing a little deducing of my own."

Pleasure blanketed Max's face.

"It's Bibi."

"Nice kid."

"Yes. I think so too. It may be why Tippy needs five hundred dollars."

"What do you mean?"

"It's something a woman would notice right away and I noticed back at the Cloven Hoof."

Max waited.

"And that's why maybe Tippy needed five hundred dollars and Bibi's going home to Chicago. I think she's pregnant."

CHAPTER ELEVEN

Max's mouth was open but not a sound emerged. The waiter brought the sandwiches and the coffee, and as soon as his back was turned, Sylvia bit into hers and munched contentedly.

"It's good," she said as she masticated. "Eat something. Look how you look."

Max closed his mouth and stared at the sandwich, but he had no appetite. He looked at Sylvia. He said weakly, "I suppose it's possible."

"Of course it's possible," said Sylvia after swallowing and contemplating the next mouthful. "They're equipped."

He took a sip of his coffee, and when he replaced the cup on the saucer he did it a little too loudly.

Sylvia lowered her sandwich and studied him for a moment. "I don't believe it," she said.

"You don't believe what."

"You're *shocked.*"

"I'm just taken by surprise, that's all."

"You're *shocked,*" she repeated. "All this time you've been sitting there with your mouth open, you've been *moralizing.*"

"Nonsense!"

"Don't nonsense me! I've been with the board of education for fifteen years. I know a puritan when I see one." She dropped the remains of the sandwich on her plate and wiped her fingers with a paper napkin. "You shocked *yourself* when you did the same thing with your wife!" She'd struck a nerve and she knew it. She steeled herself and waited for the blow. None came. He was staring out the window.

"Maybe you're right," he said finally.

"Thank you," she replied.

"For what?"

"For not chickening out. I was afraid you were going to let me have it. Most men don't like it when women call their shots. In a way," she said and began to chuckle, "it's kind of charming. A new-world fellow with old-world ideas. Was your old man a bluenose?"

"That's as good a word as any."

"You didn't think much of bastards until Tippy, did you?"

He managed a smile. "You a witch or something?"

"To most of my kids, yes. Eat your sandwich. There's nothing so depressing as cold pastrami."

Max took a bite. There was nothing so depressing as this sandwich. He put it back on the plate and leaned back, making the effort to chew and swallow the portion in his mouth. He took more coffee.

"I suppose Tippy rates because he writes poetry," said Sylvia. "It appeals to the esthete in you. Or maybe the poems make it easier to understand and appreciate him. It's too bad your son didn't write poetry, and I could *kill* myself for saying it." She shut her eyes tightly, face agonizing, waiting for the blow she felt she deserved.

What she received was totally unexpected, a memory to be treasured for the rest of her life. He caressed her cheek affectionately. She opened her eyes, reached up and patted his hand.

"Thank you. Like all teachers, I'm an armchair psychiatrist. Of course, I hate it in anybody else. But it was right there on top and I had to say it. I could have cut my tongue in two but there would've been plenty left. Big mouths and big tongues. A Steinberg trait. My maiden name when I was a maiden. Eat your sandwich."

"I can't."

"Well, I'm happy to tell you I'm finished and it was delicious. Want to go to the Cloven Hoof and corroborate my theory?"

"First I want to try Lois Corey again. If Wilma Blaney's there, she may have a lead on Marcus."

"I don't know how you do it."

"Do what?"

"Look for missing persons. It must be heartbreaking."

"Sometimes."

He fished in his pocket for a coin and crossed to the phone booth and dialed Lois' number.

Sylvia Plotkin admired his broad shoulders and strong back as he walked away from the table. (A good man, she thought. Even better than he thinks he is, and when will I learn to think before I talk?)

There was nothing much Marcus could do about the bloodstains on his jacket and his shirt, but his face was clean and the cut had clotted. (Stinking dago bitch.

Whore and sister of a whore. I'll break every bone in your body, tear every muscle in your arms, break every heel on your shoes. Then I'll go out looking for that kid myself and break every bone in *his* body. And for good measure I might beat up Lois Laura . . .)

His train of thought clotted.

Leaving the john, his line of vision connected with a headline and a photograph on the front page of the first evening edition of the *Daily News* a barfly was reading. It was the beautiful face as he had first known it three years ago. It would never look that way again. The headline said she was dead. Murdered.

He grabbed the edge of the cigarette machine to keep from keeling over. (So this is how it is when everything closes in. Okay. So this is how it is. The farewell blues . . . But I ain't going alone.)

In the coffee bar, Wilma ordered her third espresso. She watched impatiently for Van Larsen through the grimy window and tried to ignore the beatnik at the next table, with the tobacco-stained yellow beard, the oversized green sweater, the too-tight jeans that emphasized his assets, and the dirty fingernails, who tried four times to strike up a conversation. There was no point in moving to another table. The joint was too small.

At his fifth attempt to socialize, she turned to him and snapped, "Beat it, sonny." He grinned, and like his sweater, his teeth were oversized and green.

(Dear God, thought Wilma grimly, you're so good to me lately.)

Lois hung up the phone, crossed to the window, and sat looking out, her face frozen in resignation. (Let Van Larsen go to Wilma and get a statement from her about Marcus and the *paisanos.* Let Marcus be destroyed, if not by the government, then by his confederates. He is of no use to anyone any longer. Maybe I'm not either. Destroy. Destruction. What those kids on the street are protesting against. They're young enough for that. I'm not any longer. Be found, Tippy, and live your life as you choose. Come to me, Basil, and we'll grow old together. I want calm, serenity and peace. Just once before I die, let me look like a madonna.

That filthy old man out there in the pink and yellow toga with the crown of leaves on his head and that staff in his hand and that stuffed bird on his wrist looks like a goddamn fool—and doesn't that cop see the old bugger's annoying that little girl who looks so adorable as Little Red Riding Hood. Hit him, kid. Hit the old lecher with your little yellow basket.)

"Back tho thoon?" Satan greeted Max and Sylvia gleefully.

The expression on his face was as absurd as admission prices to East Side movie theaters.

"Our crowd hath thinned down thome," Satan continued, wetting the tips of two fingers and running them up his left horn. "Where would you like to thit?"

Max and Sylvia were gazing past his horns to the rear of the room, searching for Bibi. Max was trying to understand why the immutability of Lois' voice disturbed him when she had relayed Wilma's message five minutes ago.

Sylvia was praying her intuition hadn't failed her as to Bibi's pregnancy.

Bibi saw them first. She was sitting alone at a rear table, sipping a cup of tea. Her costume tail hung limply over the back of her chair. She placed her elbows on the table, interwove her hands and rested her chin on them. Her face betrayed no emotion. She waited patiently for the hunters to flush their quarry.

"There she is," said Sylvia, tugging at Max's sleeve. "She sees us."

Satan had traced Sylvia's eyeline to Bibi.

"Well!" he simpered. "Ithn't Mith Bibi the popular one!"

(And to think, thought Max, I used to be amused by Franklin Pangborn.)

He laid his hand gently on Satan's shoulder.

Satan's eyes lit up as hope sprung eternal at the unexpected gesture. "Yeth?"

"Jaywalk."

Bibi smiled at the approaching couple. There was a chair for Sylvia, and Max confiscated one from an adjoining table for himself.

"Would you like something to drink?" asked Bibi. "On me."

Max shook his head, and Sylvia's lips formed "No, thanks" though no sound emerged.

Max plunged right in. "Miss Plotkin thinks you're pregnant. Is that so?"

Bibi unfolded her hands and sat up stiffly. "So what?"

"Is it Tippy's baby?" asked Max.

"Yes."

"Was the five hundred for an abortion?"

"Yes."

"Then you know if he got the money. You've seen him since Sunday morning."

"No," said Bibi, "and no. I want the baby."

Sylvia's face was wreathed with the sort of sentimental smile only the sound of a distant lullaby could inspire. Max hoped she wouldn't burst into tears. She didn't. She reached over and patted Bibi's hand. It was ice-cold.

"If Tippy knew you wanted the baby," pressed Max, "then why the frantic search for the money?"

"Well, in the first place, when I told him about the baby, he asked me to marry him." She smiled. "When you give it enough thought, the idea's a bit silly. He's seventeen, I'm twenty-two, and what's there to hold us together except the baby? Besides, I told you, I'm not in love with him. I didn't decide to go home until Monday. I called my mother in Chicago. I laid the situation on the line to her and believe it or not she took it beautifully. So I'm going home."

She took a sip of her tea while Sylvia decided there was hope for Bibi's generation.

"When I tried to phone Tippy," continued Bibi, "that's when I learned he was missing. I thought he might have run away"—she shrugged—"because of our situation. You see, I could never agree to an abortion. In the first place, it's against my religion. And in the second place, I want the baby."

"Regardless of what people say?" said Max.

Bibi cocked an eyebrow as she stared at Max quizzically. "You must be kidding. In this age of enlightenment?" The statement was both crisp and wry. "I must say, the idea of fathering a bastard didn't appeal to Tippy either. In fact, he got a bit violent about it. I guess it touched an exposed nerve. We had a row Sunday morning and Tippy went rampaging out of my place. Honestly, that's the last I've seen of him."

(An exposed nerve, thought Max. The truth about himself the exposed nerve.)

"Mr. Van Larsen."

He looked into Bibi's direct, honest eyes.

"If he's gone away, I don't think he did without first trying to wipe some slates clean. He did a lot of yelling about bastards and gangsters and junkies and whores and the Blaneys . . . and his Aunt Lois."

(Lois the immutable.)

"Do you need any money?" asked Max suddenly.

"No, thanks," said Bibi with a Mona Lisa smile, "but thanks."

"Listen, honey," said Sylvia impulsively, "I teach at Wagner High. Do me a favor. Drop me an announcement. I'd like to know if it's a boy or a girl. Would you do that?"

Bibi nodded. "I won't forget." Solemnly she shook hands with Max and Sylvia, who resisted an urge to bend over and kiss her cheek. She hoped it would be a boy.

After the cab driver deposited Marcus at the edge of the crowd, he came to one of his rare immediate decisions. The guy had been talking to himself all the way from the bar to the block party. Most of it was in Italian but enough of it told him there was going to be trouble. What with the cut on his head and the bloodstains on his clothes . . . and he was positive the guy was carrying a rod and he decided to hunt up a cruising patrol car or if necessary drive to the nearest precinct. If he fingered a killer, Shirley the wife could really lord it over her mah-jongg club.

Max guided Sylvia through the crush on Bleecker Street. There were no taxis cruising and he was anxious to get to Wilma Blaney. He wondered what progress Roper was making at his end.

"Where are you taking me?" asked Sylvia.

"Wilma Blaney, or have you had enough?"

"Listen, if I'm no hindrance to your progress, I prefer to stay with you." (Until death do us part, if you were reasonable.) "I'm getting the education I never got at Hunter College."

He squeezed her arm affectionately, and Sylvia began to feel giddy. She gulped air, swallowing traces of pizza smells and beatnik smells and gasoline fumes, and yet it all tasted sweet to her palate.

Once off Bleecker Street, Max reluctantly slackened his pace. He could tell by the frantic clicking of Sylvia's heels that she was struggling to keep up with him.

"My poor little poet," puffed Sylvia, "he's sure been going through a crash course in living. Do you suppose" —Max's profile out of the corner of her eye too set, too tightly drawn, too anxious—"all this might have in some way, God forbid, unbalanced him?"

"Possible."

"I have a nephew who married at eighteen. He got a girl pregnant too. It's the new virus, I guess. But they're very happy. They have a darling apartment in Kew Gardens."

"I'd like to wring somebody's neck," said Max through clenched teeth.

Sylvia grabbed his arm. The look on his face frightened her. They stopped walking and faced each other.

"Listen, Max, it's none of my business . . . *but* . . ."

His fingers were working, but not as swiftly as Sylvia's tongue.

". . . your job is to find the boy, not pass judgment on the people who've fouled up his life. It's nice to know that your soul's defrosting and you're relating to Tippy. But as far as his people are concerned, take a tip from Shakespeare, William . . . leave them to heaven. I'm no armchair analyst, because I happen to be standing at the moment, but I think you got all the grief you can handle. You want to hit me or something, or shall I go home and bite my tongue for the rest of the night, or what?"

They stared at each other for approximately thirty seconds, and then Max kissed her cheek.

(I'll never wash this cheek again, thought Sylvia, never. Either that or I make a wax impression.)

Max took her hand and they hastened to find Wilma Blaney.

The Prince of Darkness was climbing the ladder to the trapdoor to the roof. His face was covered with filth, his hair matted with bits of straw and plaster, the black cloak torn in three places. There had been fragments of a broken mirror on the floor of the loft and he'd caught a jagged reflection of himself.

(*I can pass a person on the street . . . and my eyes meet theirs . . . and I see it . . .*

See what?

The death look.)

His spindly fingers with their broken nails were no match for the trapdoor. He pushed weakly, then clawed feebly. He lowered his head, climbed another rung, and heaved his shoulders against the rotting square barrier. Slowly it began to give.

Five teen-agers on the roof of the derelict building were lighting firecrackers and cherry bombs and flinging them at the crowd below.

"Hey!" yelled one triumphantly. "I just hit a dike!"

The three boys and two girls whooped and yelled and howled with glee and the policemen on the street below decided the hell with them. They had enough to do keeping order in the crowd. Their latest victim was pushing her way home through the crowd to get her air rifle.

The trapdoor tore open and Ashley Junior's frightening apparition of a face appeared. The first to see him was one of the girls, and her terrified shriek alerted her four companions. The second girl added a shriek to her friend's, and then one of the boys made it a trio, and the five took to their heels and escaped to the adjoining roof, the building in which Lois Corey resided.

The Prince of Darkness crawled onto the roof, struggled to his feet and crossed slowly to the edge. Exhausted, he sat down to rest. He found matches, some firecrackers, and a half-empty box of sparklers.

"*Tippy!*" he whispered. "*Remember last Fourth of July? Remember how we lit sparklers and ran through the graveyard demanding the dead awaken? Remember, Tippy?*"

He fumbled with the matches and then lit a sparkler. It fizzled and sputtered and then came to life, and for the first time in months the Prince of Darkness laughed.

Her fifth espresso, in which a limp piece of lemon peel floated, was ice-cold. Equally cold were her fingers as she fumbled in her purse for her compact and lipstick.

Green Teeth's grimy hands were playing up and down the insides of his thighs insinuatingly.

Disgusting creep, thought Wilma, as she lavished her lips with two swift smears of carmine.

(Get here, Van Larsen. Get here fast before my resolve begins to weaken. I'm less angry and less brave than I was an hour ago. I'm thinking of Mario and what he'll do to me when he finds out what I've told you, if you ever get here and I can tell you, before I run out of here and into the car and drive God knows where until I decide what to do with the rest of my lousy life.

Hurry, Van Larsen. Maybe Mario got to Lois before you did. Maybe he's beaten my whereabouts out of her.)

She touched the nailfile in her purse reassuringly. Wilma heard Green Teeth stirring behind her. Without turning her head, she felt him leaning toward her. Her fingers tightened around the nailfile.

The block party had reached bacchanalian heights. Marcus stood at the edge of the crowd, staring at the lighted windows of Lois Corey's apartment. He could see her sitting in one of the windows, reading. He touched his jacket. The small automatic was resting snugly in his inside breast pocket.

"Make way! Make way!" commanded the voice majestically.

"Watch who you're shoving!" snarled Marcus.

He was rewarded with a magnanimous smile from the large woman with the beautiful face, the jet-black hair pulled back into a tight, neat bun, the jingling earrings, a flowing purple cape, and a briefcase under her arm.

"I do not shove," said Madame Vilna with an imperious wave of her hand. "I merely gesture you to one side. I am the entertainment," pointing to the speaker's platform, "and I am late!" She elbowed her way into the crowd, head held high like a show horse who knew all the prizes would be hers.

Still scowling, Marcus cursed under his breath and smoothed his jacket sleeve. A chubby blond girl wearing a bikini and a mask that was slightly larger edged next to him and whispered in his ear, "My name is Charity." Her hand caressed his thigh. "I begin at home."

"Buzz off, you turd," snarled Marcus and pushed his way into the crowd.

There were costumes and masks both bizarre and simple. There were teen-agers, middle-agers and over-agers both bizarre and simple. Someone stuck the soft end of a feather in his ear and he roughly slapped the hand away. He passed a couple locked in a tight embrace and kissing passionately.

He heard a policeman yell at the couple, "Break it up, you guys!"

Marcus bumped into a wizened old crone carrying a placard that read CUBA, SI, SEX, NO.

On the speaker's platform, three professional couples were executing the watusi in frenzy and abandonment to the accompaniment of a five-piece band.

More placards flashed before Marcus' eyes.

END THE WAR IN VIET NAM

BETTER RED THAN DEAD

CAPITALISM IS DESTRUCTION

PULL OUT OF VIET NAM

I DIDN'T RAISE MY BOY TO BE A SOLDIER

L.B.J. . . . OY VAY

Madame Vilna introduced herself to the chairman of the block party committee, an intense young man with an Ish Kabibble haircut, steel-rimmed glasses, and Sen-Sen breath. "I am Vilna!"

The young man clasped her hand and smiled a rabbit's-tooth smile. "You follow the dancers, Madame Vilna. It may be a bit of an ordeal, I'm afraid. It's gotten a bit out of hand."

Madame Vilna drew herself up to her full stature. "Leave it to Vilna."

Green Teeth howled and was astonished to see blood seeping from the slash on his wrist.

Wilma leaped to her feet, tugged the door open, and ran out.

Not a patron in the coffee bar stirred.

"She pay you?" the owner asked the waitress.

"Yeah."

Green Teeth, blazing with anger, pushed the table aside and sprang for the door.

Wilma ran to the car lot and the safety of her automobile. *Damn Van Larsen! Damn Mario! Damn Lois! Damn Tippy! Damn everybody!* As she ran, she fumbled in her purse for her keys. The heel of the shoe caught on the edge of the curb and she went sprawling face-down onto the sidewalk.

Her scream tore through the air as Green Teeth grabbed her arms and pulled her to her feet. She beat at his face with her fists. His right fist was headed for her chin when he suddenly howled in agony.

Max held the fist in a viselike grip, spun him around and swiftly sent his knee into Green Teeth's midriff. Green Teeth's face contorted in agony as Max delivered a fist to his nose. Green Teeth crumpled to the sidewalk.

Sylvia had her arms around the hysterical Wilma, whose face was buried in Sylvia's ample bosom.

Max was looking around for a policeman, but there wasn't one. He kicked Green Teeth in the ribs. "Get up!" He kicked him again. "Get up, you filth!"

Green Teeth struggled to his knees. Max pulled him to his feet, slapped his face, then with a rough shove sent him on his way.

"There, there," purred Sylvia, patting Wilma's back

gently, like a mother trying to burp a baby. "There, there."

Wilma raised her tear-stained face and looked into the sympathetic eyes. Then slowly she swiveled her neck and focused on Max. Her face contorted with rage. "What the hell kept *you?*"

CHAPTER TWELVE

"Rotten jungle!" Wilma's voice trembled and trebled. "That's what this city is, a dog-eat-dog rotten jungle."

(And you exemplify a certain type of animal, thought Max.)

They were sitting in her parked car, Wilma in the front seat behind the wheel, Max next to her, Sylvia in the back. Her eyes greeted Wilma's.

"I know you," said Wilma.

Sylvia selected the open-school-week smile. "I'm Miss Plotkin, one of Tippy's teachers. We've met before and spoke on the phone."

"I thought so."

"Where's your husband?" asked Max.

"In hell, I hope." She was repairing her face in the rear-view mirror. "Maybe with Lois. Maybe on the lam. Maybe dead, but not the way my luck's been running." She turned to Max with a vicious smile. "He's *kaput*, baby. Washed up. The boys have put the finger on him. They're closing the warehouse, the auction rooms, and Marcus. He's too hot."

(Wait till you hear how the heat's increased, thought Max.)

She chuckled grimly. "If Tippy only knew how well he's succeeded."

"Is this what you wanted to tell me?"

"There's more, handsome, plenty more."

Sylvia shifted and crossed her legs. Would she hold forth in the teachers' lunchroom tomorrow!

"Well?" Max prodded Wilma impatiently.

"We lied about the last time we saw Tippy."

Max wondered if they heard his heart accelerate.

"We saw him Sunday night, when we got back to town. He was in the house when we got there, tearing his room apart. Just out of anger, that's all. Sheer anger. He'd apparently had a blistering fight with somebody before he came home. He told us he knew everything. Told us he'd seen Lois and let her have it too. He began chewing out Marcus and me and then told Marcus about some poem he'd written about him which spilled the beans about the *paisanos* and a few other untidy items concerning the warehouse.

"Then he said if Marcus didn't give him the five hundred dollars, he'd send the poem off to that damned magazine with a copy to the police or the F.B.I., I forget which, not that it matters, and ahhh . . . it was terrible. He was shrieking like a stuck pig, a hysterical woman. Marcus started slapping him around."

She was raising a cigarette to her lips. Max tore it from her fingers and flung it out the window. Wilma's face drained and her eyes were filled with new fear.

"Come on! Come on! Finish it!" Max could feel his control slowly ebbing and fought desperately to contain himself.

Wilma started talking again, two octaves higher. "Well, like I told you! He started slapping the kid around! He wanted to know who in the warehouse had finked on him! Who was slipping Tippy the figurines! But Tippy just laughed, like a little hyena, he just laughed! He kept going *hee-haw hee-haw* over and over again, and Marcus kept getting redder and redder. Then Tippy picked up that damn tin box of his and threw it at Marcus. Marcus ducked and the damn thing almost hit *me!*"

(Too bad, thought Sylvia.)

"Then Marcus jumped him and they were struggling on the floor and I kept begging them both to cut it! The next thing I know, Marcus has Tippy by the neck and is banging his head on the floor . . . *don't look at me like that.*"

Max's right hand was clutching the wheel, his left jammed against the back of the seat. "The rest!" he snapped. "Give me the rest!"

"Well . . . well . . ." She fumbled in terror. "I ran to Marcus to pull him off the kid and he reaches out and takes a swat at *me*. That's when Tippy got loose. He poked Marcus in the eye. Then, then he called me a dirty name, picked up the tin box, and ran out of the house. That's the God's honest truth."

"And that's the last you've seen him?"

"Yes, yes, so help me, yes."

"And that cock-and-bull of your husband's about seeing Tippy in Washington Square?"

"He made it up."

Sylvia's lower lip ached. She realized she'd been biting it.

Max found his control. "That's why you waited so long to report Tippy missing. Marcus didn't want him found."

"Yes, he did!" she cried. "He really did." (Why am I

defending the son of a bitch? I hate his guts.) "He realized it was important to find the kid and make peace with him and . . ."

". . . And what?"

". . . And find out what was going on in the warehouse he didn't know about."

"Antonia Burgess was murdered."

Wilma gasped.

Max gave her the details. "Marcus is our number-one suspect. It won't be too easy on you either."

"Listen!" She grabbed one of his lapels. "I want to turn state's evidence against Marcus, only you got to promise me protection. It's not just him, it's the others. Antonia. Oh God, I'm frightened. Marcus almost killed *me* tonight too! I know where he keeps the books. *All* the books. I know where he keeps everything. I know the names in Italy . . ."

(Well, fumed Sylvia inwardly, Tippy certainly didn't learn loyalty from *you,* you Neapolitan *nafke.*)

"Marcus is out looking for you." Max relished the torture in her eyes. "One of your neighbors called the cops and saw him go chasing after you."

"He may be with Lois," she squeaked. "He'll make her tell him where I am."

"Then let's us go to Lois," said Max. (And God help Marcus Blaney when I lay my hands on him.)

"Please! Please! People! *Please!"*

The intense young man with the Ish Kabibble haircut popped his *p*'s into the microphone and they exploded out of the loudspeaker and drifted into nothingness in a harmless fallout.

Madame Vilna stood behind him, a proud, commanding, dignified figure that demanded attention. The demand went unheeded. The intense young man signaled the band for a fanfare and got one. It received the same attention from the milling crowd a television commercial gets from a viewer rummaging in the refrigerator.

"Step aside," said Madame Vilna.

The chairman abdicated his position and Madame Vilna stepped to the microphone.

"Let . . . us . . . now . . . prayyyyy."

Five hundred heads swiveled in her direction. That was about two-thirds of the crowd. Madame Vilna led them in a prayer. She was prepared at its conclusion to swoop directly into a poem. *Hold them while you got them.* In her mind rang the immortal words of the late Jewish tragedian Jacob P. Adler.

Marcus stood near a pretzel vendor, waiting for the policeman to move away from Lois' stoop. He could see her still sitting in the window.

The words coming over the loudspeaker sounded like a prayer. His eyes darted to the speaker's platform. He saw the big broad who had jostled him earlier. *Some entertainment . . . a crummy prayer.*

The twelve-year-old girl dressed as a fairy, in a sweet costume made of muslin and gauze with two cardboard wings attached at the shoulders, lifted her wand and brought it crashing down on the head of the old man in the pink and yellow toga whose hand was under her dress. Then she screamed at the top of her lungs, "He's touching me dirty! He's touching me dirty!" and a dozen heads shot around, sized up the situation, and boiled with outrage.

Clifton Southford tried to fight his way past them, but a grimy hand with a bloodstained handkerchief wrapped around the wrist had him collared and was pounding on his head with the other hand. He saw his assailant was wearing an oversized green sweater and had disgusting olive-green teeth . . . his mouth was parted and spitting epithets like buckshot.

Fingers clawed at his face and Southford made feeble efforts to free himself. Somebody yelled for a cop, and the policeman standing at the foot of Lois' stoop rushed toward the melee and Marcus Blaney took advantage of his opportunity and bounded up the steps into the vestibule.

Clifton Southford sank to his knees under the rain of blows, clawing fingers, and kicking feet, and the little twelve-year-old fairy found her mother and asked her to please buy her a Good Humor like she promised. Green Teeth's foot connected with Southford's left ear. The sculptor groaned and collapsed just as the policeman arrived, pushing people aside roughly, then knelt beside Southford's prostrated body.

"He's a dirty sex fiend!" yelled Green Teeth indignantly, and from behind him someone yelled, "String him up!"

The policeman blew his whistle for reinforcements.

Lois Corey stared at the door, the knob shaking violently.

"Go away, Marcus."

"Let me in, damn it. I won't hurt you."

"I'm not afraid of you."

"Then let me in."

"Go away."

"Where's *Wilma!*"

"I don't know."

"Let me *in.*"

"Go away."

"After all I did for you! After all I did for you and your kid!"

"God will repay you."

His scatalogical comment on God made her cringe.

"Ground into dust on battlefields
In strange and alien lands . . ."

(I got them, Jacob P. darling, and I'm holding them.) Madame Vilna's hands were clenched in supplication. Her head was lifted upward, her eyes focusing on a patch of sky just beyond the roof of the derelict building on the opposite side of the street.

"Torn from earth, too soon too soon,
Torn from outstretched hands . . ."

"Hey, lady!" yelled a teen-ager jiggling his crotch obscenely. "Tear this!"

(Oh boy, thought Rodriguez, if I ever tried this on Plotkin!)

"Tippy's back!" cried Marcus desperately through the door. "He's back, I tell you, and he's sick!"

"You're lying."

"So help me, Lois. So help me! He came home right after Wilma left. He's in bed. He wants *you!*"

"You're lying! You're lying!"

"What the hell kind of a mother are you? Ain't you done enough to that kid? You want to die with another sin on your head?"

Lois unlocked the door.

Marcus leaped into the room, waving the automatic, slammed the door shut, and leaned against it.

"Okay, you miserable whore . . . *where is she?*"

The attendants placed Clifton Southford on the stretcher, lifted it and carried it through an aisle cleared by the police. A woman spat at Southford as the stretcher went past her and a little angel licking a Good Humor and fingering the crisp five-dollar bill in her pocket giggled.

From the opposite direction of the street, Max held tightly to Wilma Blaney's arm with one hand; the other held tightly to Sylvia Plotkin. With the aid of two patrolmen they were forcing their way to Lois Corey's building.

"Supposing he's got his gun!" pleaded Wilma desperately.

"He won't use it."

"You don't know him!"

"I know him."

"Gaping wounds never to heal,
Eyes from their sockets torn . . ."

From the corner of his eye Max espied Madame Vilna declaiming, and for the first time in over an hour he smiled.

"Hey, Plotkin! Hey, Plotkin! Over here!"

Sylvia winced. She had spotted Rodriguez waving at her. "Go home and do your homework!" she yelled. "Or tomorrow . . . *deportation!*"

"Haw!" snorted Rodriguez as he poked a friend in the ribs with his elbow. "Over dere . . . my teacher . . . Plotkin!" He added with pride, "What a crazy piece!"

"I don't know where she is." Lois took pride in her composure.

(I shall never be disturbed again.)

"Putana."

"Go away, Marcus. The police are after you. Wilma's with Van Larsen."

(But is she? Has he gotten to her? Where are you, Basil?)

"Where?"

The menace in his voice did nothing to ruffle her composure. She was enjoying her game of cat-and-mouse with the ugly little man and his ugly little gun.

"It doesn't matter even if I told you. They're together

now. I delivered her message to him a long time ago. I hope you roast in hell."

He lunged forward and caught her across the mouth with the back of his hand.

Green Teeth stepped swiftly behind two burly characters swilling beer from cans when he spotted the patrolmen making a path to Lois' building for Max and the two women. He watched their struggle through the mob in front of the derelict building and chuckled at the desperate look on Wilma's face.

"My name is Charity," whispered a voice in his ear, "and I begin at home."

He turned his head slowly, sized up the bikini-clad figure with a professional eye, smiled his green smile and winked.

As she reached the last four lines of Tippy's poem, Madame Vilna's passion boiled and bubbled and threatened to erupt.

Her eyes remained focused on that patch of sky just beyond the roof of the derelict building, when suddenly into her line of vision, standing on the edge of the roof, appeared a tiny black figure with a billowing cape, holding in each outstretched hand a lighted sparkler.

The tiny black figure was staring into the void and swaying.

Madame Vilna's voice faltered.

"Tippy," wept the Prince of Darkness, *"Tippy!"*

Madame Vilna's shriek amplified its way through the air and attacked every pair of ears on the street. Heads shot in her direction. She stood with hand outstretched and face etched with horror, pointing to the roof of the derelict building. All heads turned and saw the Prince of Darkness with his billowing cloak and his dazzling sparklers, and a sudden, expectant hush fell over the street.

Sylvia Plotkin squinted at the roof. Max's eyes widened in recognition. Wilma shoved a fist against her mouth.

"Tippy-y-y-y-y-y-y . . ."

The Prince of Darkness leaped into space, the sparklers sputtering and dying before he did. The cloak billowed out behind him, and for a brief moment he resembled a giant bat swooping down for the attack.

There were screams, there were groans, there were shouts, there were yells, there were tears, and there was Sylvia Plotkin covering her eyes and crying, "Oh my God, it's Whatsisname!"

CHAPTER THIRTEEN

Ashley Tybor Junior, the Prince of Darkness, Whatsisname, lay in a broken black heap on the pavement.

A patrolman barked into a call box for an ambulance.

Sylvia Plotkin wept uncontrollably as Max kneeled beside the body and turned Ashley Tybor over on his back.

There was a beautiful smile on his face.

Gently Max untied the cloak, lifted Ashley slightly to pull the cloak from under him, and then covered his body. He got to his feet and spoke to one of the policemen. "I know the kid. His name's Ashley Tybor Junior. Senior owns a mortuary on Bowery and Delancey. Call there. They can probably locate him for you."

The remaining police struggled to control the crowd.

"Move back!" yelled Max. "Move back! This isn't a circus!"

(It's a jungle, thought Wilma, filled with stinking animals.)

They heard sirens in the distance, and Max nodded with relief to one of the patrolmen.

The roofs of the building were filling again with the curious jockeying for a better look at the body. There were too many people on the roof of the derelict building and a patrolman blew his whistle and tried to warn them off. A cherry bomb exploded.

The squad car pulled up at the edge of the crowd and Roper was the first to emerge. (That cabbie's tip better not be a false alarm. Nice guy. Had a paperback copy of *Call It Sleep* in his jacket pocket.)

In Lois' apartment, Marcus stood near the window, staring out at the mob congesting the entrance to the building, and cursed. Lois sat behind the sewing machine, face still smarting from Marcus' blow, attempting to reassemble what was left of her composure. Marcus could see Max and Wilma, and his anger boiled up anew. Max was pushing through toward Lois' stoop.

(Let them come, thought Marcus, let them come. I'll take the two of them with this gun. It'll be beautiful. Beautiful.) "They're coming," he croaked in a half-whisper, "they're coming. Wilma and the detective. They're here."

He shifted the automatic from his left hand to his right, and wiped the palm of the left on his trousers.

The sirens were drawing closer and the frog's palms were getting sweatier. He shifted the gun back to his left hand and wiped the palm of his right on his jacket. It moistened one of the caked bloodstains and his hand was now tinged with red. Lois could see Max Van Larsen ascending the stoop. Her mouth was dry. Her skin was clammy. (I've seen too much death in my lifetime. Too much. Enough. No more.)

Slowly she worked her hand to the knob of a drawer in the sewing machine.

Slowly, praying warped wood wouldn't grind against warped wood, she opened the drawer. She moved her hand into the drawer and her fingers closed around the familiar shape of the pinking shears.

Max hesitated on the top step of the stoop. (Hadn't Lois Corey heard the commotion? Could she remain that oblivious to the screaming and yelling that accompanied the Prince of Darkness' suicide? Marcus Blaney has a gun. If he's in there with her, he might be poised to use it. *You don't know Marcus.*)

Two patrolmen stood tensely at the foot of the stoop.

Sylvia Plotkin nibbled nervously at a cuticle, and Wilma Blaney wished she knew a formula for disappearing into thin air. (Does that nonsense still hold good, she wondered, about a wife not being able to testify against her husband? I'll get a Mexican divorce, she resolved—I could use a rest—and *then* testify. I'll need some jazzy new clothes for the trial.)

Wilma screamed, and Sylvia Plotkin, trained in the art of ducking flying erasers and chalk ends, dropped to her knees. Max drew his revolver and motioned the others to stand back.

The pinking shears had come crashing through the window and landed with a clatter on the pavement.

Marcus spun around, frog eyes blinking rapidly in momentary bewilderment, and shot wild in the general direction of Lois.

(I am calm. I am serene. I am peaceful.)

She sat with her hands in her lap. The smile on her face was blissfully beatific. A madonna. Behind her, the bullet had torn through the sampler on the wall.

(The family that prays together stays together.)

Marcus panicked.

He rushed for the door, tore it open, entered the hall, fired one shot blindly at the door to the street, then headed up the stairs to the roof.

The bullet crashed through the door glass, whistled past Max, and fortunately found no target.

Madame Vilna clasped her hands, shouted *"Cossacks!"* and then dwelt for a few moments on her brilliant Natasha in Tolstoi's *Resurrection.*

Max kicked the vestibule door open, motioned the patrolmen to follow him, raced into the hall and up the stairs.

On the first-floor landing Marcus crashed into two garbage pails and went sprawling to the floor. He scrambled to his knees, and through the banister railing fired another shot.

It crashed into a hall panel just above Max's head, striking a faded painted satyr in the left buttock. Max didn't return the fire.

"You're wasting good ammunition, Blaney!" he shouted. "Throw the gun down here and then follow it!"

"Up *you!*" Marcus rushed for the next landing.

In the street, Roper deployed some men to reach the roof through another building. "Damn it," he muttered to himself. "Blaney's my department."

The curious were being cleared from the roof of Lois' building by a policeman. A kid yelled, "Oh boy!" Another shouted, "It's better than TV!" And the rest had the good sense to rush for safety. Eight took the direction that led over the roof of the derelict building, and one yelled for help when his foot went through a hole in the ceiling. Two pulled him to safety as that portion of the roof sagged.

The policeman positioned himself behind a smokestack. It was only a small smokestack, actually a chimney guilty of imposture, but he'd seen movie cops do it and he trusted the minimum protection it afforded him.

Marcus crouched against the door leading to the roof. From that position he figured he had command of the situation.

Max hoped somebody had the brains to send some cops up to the roof.

Roper hoped one of his trigger-happy cops wouldn't shoot Max by mistake.

On the pavement outside, Sylvia Plotkin closed her eyes and recited to herself the Jewish prayer for the dead: "*Vay ish kadahl vay ish kaddish . . .*"

Wilma Blaney was making plans for her widowhood.

Lois Corey had come out on the stoop, was staring at the cape-covered corpse. "Who is it?" she asked no one in particular.

"Just some crazy show-off, lady!" a coarse voice shouted, and Sylvia Plotkin's eyes flew open, narrowed into ominous slits, and searched for Rodriguez.

Max and the two patrolmen edged slowly along the third-floor hall. "Blaney?"

Marcus tightened his grip on the automatic.

"You're a damn fool, Blaney. You're locked in. There

are cops on the roof." (I hope.) "Throw the gun down. Which do you prefer? Us or your *paisanos?*"

"I don't care any more," croaked the frog.

(You wouldn't, thought Max. A kid meant nothing to you, Antonia Burgess meant nothing to you . . . why should your rotten life? But don't get yourself killed, Frog. Please God, those cops on the roof, if there are cops on the roof, shouldn't be trigger-happy. I want the pleasure of roughing-up Marcus Blaney. I want to feel my fist crashing into his amphibian's face. I want to knock him to the ground and grab his throat and bang his head mercilessly the way he did Tippy.)

Quietly Marcus unlatched the door to the roof. He straightened up cautiously, sent two shots roaring down the stairwell, then rushed onto the roof.

Roper's deployment was emerging four roofs away as the cop behind the chimney leaped to his feet, took aim, and Marcus' sixth shot caught him in the right shoulder. The cop's gun dropped before he did. Marcus rushed blindly past him to the roof of the derelict building. Roper's men were taking aim when Max came tearing onto the roof, firing a shot over Marcus' head.

A wailing siren was on top of them as the ambulance arrived on the scene.

Marcus made it over the roof divider as Max came racing up behind him. The frog was midway across the derelict roof when Max's flying tackle caught him around the ankles and both went crashing to the floor. The roof groaned, Marcus shrieked in agony, several policemen shouted warnings to Max as the weakened portion of the derelict roof sagged and parted.

Max and Marcus disappeared through the hole and

crashed to the floor below, landing on a packing case that gave way beneath their weight.

Heavy clouds of dust and filth clogged Max's nostrils and mouth. He had landed on something soft, and though his body ached, he didn't think any bones were broken. He blessed the soft object that had cushioned his fall.

It was the only time he would ever bless Marcus Blaney.

Several patrolmen clambered through the trapdoor and down the ladder into the loft. All gagged at the revoltingly disgusting odor of decay permeating the place. All drew their revolvers. Two got to Max Van Larsen and pulled him away from Marcus Blaney, whose head was being banged on the floor like a hammer driving a nail.

Madame Vilna had managed to push her way through to the area occupied by Sylvia, Wilma, and Lois. She remembered then she had left her briefcase back at the speaker's platform. She mentioned it to a policeman, who promised to retrieve it for her, but somehow it didn't seem to matter that much whether he did or didn't.

Marcus Blaney lay on the floor, weeping.

"My head . . . my head," he repeated agonizedly, then, aware of an even more intense pain, "My leg! My leg!"

Roper came up behind Max. "Glad you kept him alive for me."

Max was staring at Marcus' left leg and noted with satisfaction that it was twisted grotesquely at the ankle. It rested against an object that looked like a tin box.

Max knelt and lifted the box. He wiped the heavy layer of dust from the top with his jacket sleeve. It was a candy box. His fingers fumbled anxiously as he pried open the lid.

The box was filled with some snapshots, some coins, a rosary, a photostat of a birth certificate, and a sheaf of papers neatly clipped together. Max read the name carefully lettered on the top sheet: "Henry Thorpe Blaney." Beneath the name was lettered: "Poems."

"Max? What's wrong?" Roper asked. "You're crying. Why?"

Max handed him the tin box, and like one possessed, began pushing aside packing cases and lifting crates.

"Max? What the hell's wrong with you?"

"Oh *hell!*" Max cried. "Oh, damn it to *hell!*"

Although the body was huddled in a sitting position behind two packing cases in a corner of the loft, head lowered on the chest at a grotesque angle, arms hanging limply with hands resting stiffly between the thighs, reddish brown hair fallen forward partially obscuring the face, Max could recite the corpse's identification to himself.

Henry Thorpe Blaney. Age seventeen; height, five foot eleven; weight, around one hundred and sixty . . .

He tried, but he couldn't stop the tears.

. . . Eyes brown-green; hair reddish brown; complexion, fair . . . wearing brown slacks, red sport shirt, blue blazer, white sneakers, white socks . . .

"Is it the kid?" he heard Roper ask, and nodded.

Max knelt beside Tippy. The body was rigid with rigor mortis. He brushed the hair back from the boy's face, then took a handkerchief from his pocket to wipe off the dust. He cupped his hand under Tippy's chin and knew then the neck had been broken.

In uncontrollable rage, he sent his fist crashing into a crate. It toppled over, and from it spilled a variety of objects. A copy of *Who's Who,* a small framed photograph of Bibi Dumas, several paperbacks, and a Dresden monkey that broke into several pieces when it hit the floor.

Speak no evil.

Speak no evil's pieces reposed in a little pile of white dust that had spilled from its broken interior. Max stared at the dust, then wet the tip of his finger, applied it to the white dust and transferred the finger to the tip of his tongue. He looked up at Roper through tear-misted eyes.

"Heroin. And I know who owns the other two figurines of this set."

CHAPTER FOURTEEN

Sylvia Plotkin dabbed at her eyes with a ball of Kleenex.

Madame Vilna felt a chill and drew her cape tightly around her.

Wilma Blaney anxiously waited for word that Marcus was dead.

Only Lois Corey's face was alight with joy. Basil Kirby was pushing his way through the crowd to her.

"Basil!" she cried. "Basil! You've come back!"

Basil made it to the clearing and almost stumbled over Whatsisname's body. He sidestepped nimbly and rushed to Lois' waiting arms.

"Oh, Basil, thank God," she wept. "Thank God. You don't know what I've been going through."

"Whatever it is," he said, looking into her eyes, "I've been through worse. Lois, I've lost my car . . . everything . . . my sample case, my money. The kid robbed me and took the car . . ." Lois' knees began to sag. "And I found these cops in their squad car and we chased the kid and . . . and . . . he lost control of the car and it crashed through a guard rail and oh God, Lois, it was terrible . . ."

"Tippy," she whispered. "Tippy . . ."

Basil didn't seem to hear her. "That's what you get for being a good Samaritan. That's what you get for picking up hitchhikers . . ."

"Hitchhiker!" Lois suddenly found strength again. "Oh, Basil . . . hitchhiker!"

He stared at her, dumfounded. (What's she laughing at? I've lost everything and she's laughing!)

There was a murmur from the crowd as Max emerged from the building, followed by Roper. Roper crossed to the ambulance attendants and spoke to them, and they went into the derelict building with a stretcher. Max was staring at Lois Corey in Basil Kirby's arms and wondering who the man was.

Sylvia looked at Max and whispered to herself, "Thank you, God."

Max walked past the body and the grieving parent and crossed to the women.

(He's been crying, Sylvia realized with a pang.)

Lois moved away from Basil and looked at Max. She thought he wanted to tell her something but didn't know how.

Max took a deep breath as he struggled to form words. He ran his hand wearily across his forehead and finally spoke. "I found Tippy."

Wilma paled, and Sylvia bit her lip. Madame Vilna's face lit up with joy.

Max took Lois' hand. "Don't you hear me? I said I found Tippy. He's in there. He's dead. He's probably been dead for days." (Do I tell her now he was murdered? Add another crack to the already broken heart?)

Madame Vilna felt faint and reached for Sylvia's hand.

Max was speaking again. "Found some things of his on the top floor. Some of Ashley's things too."

"Yes," Lois said softly, "it's their castle. They hid things there. When they'd get hungry, they'd come to me and I'd feed them."

(How do I tell her?)

Basil put his arm around Lois. "I'm sorry, honey. Forgive me. I should have waited. I didn't know there was trouble with Tippy."

"There isn't any longer," said Lois, and she burst into tears. Basil helped her back to the apartment.

The stretcher-bearers emerged with Marcus, and another murmur arose from the crowd.

Wilma's eyes leap-frogged to the stretcher and locked with Marcus'. "Ohhhhh, *shit!*"

Sylvia began looking for Rodriguez again before she realized the expletive was Wilma's property. She hadn't realized Max was holding her hand. She looked into his sad, tired face.

"I have to leave you," said Max. "I have to go to the precinct." He lowered his voice. "Tippy was murdered. His neck was broken."

Sylvia fought back the tears.

"Will you do me a favor? Will you break it to his mother for me? It wasn't Blaney." He emitted a ghastly chuckle. "We've already got the bastard behind bars. All we have to do is make him admit it. We'll make him admit it."

"Remember to wash your face first," said Sylvia for no accountable reason, and Max burst into uncontrollable laughter.

Edmund Cardew lay face-down on the cot, like a shipwreck in a raging sea clinging to a plank. His teeth marks made an irregular, slobbering pattern on the pillow. His legs twisted and contorted like an Indian fakir's, his torso jerking and convulsing as though under the attack of thousands of volts of electricity.

And Roper's voice was electric. "How and why did you murder Tippy Blaney and Antonia Burgess?"

The police stenographer was positive Cardew would drown in his own sea of perspiration.

Max leaned against the wall, staring down at Cardew, his face an implacable mask. Cardew lifted his head and with an effort focused his eyes again on the object Max held in his right hand. A syringe.

Max managed to speak without a trace of emotion. "We found the third Delft monkey with the H in the loft where Tippy had hidden it. Where you murdered him. The other two are in your apartment." He knew it wasn't his words that were hypnotizing Cardew. "Then there's a poem Tippy wrote incriminating you . . ." (hoping to God he could find the poem if the hophead wouldn't confess).

Cardew was sobbing. One hand gestured feebly at the syringe. The police stenographer swallowed twice and cursed himself for the midnight snack he had wolfed an hour earlier.

"The shot," begged Cardew in a voice that seemed to emanate from an echo chamber, "the shot."

Max rolled the syringe back and forth between the palms of his hands, invitingly, seductively.

Cardew's eyes traveled slowly to the police stenographer, who lowered his head like a shy virgin and swallowed again. Cardew's eyes moved back to the syringe. "I'll get the shot?"

"You'll get the shot."

The words began to ooze slowly from Cardew's mouth like drops of blood from a self-inflicted wound. The police stenographer's fingers had no trouble keeping pace with him.

"My bag isn't fifty a day. It's a hundred . . . sometimes more." Roper lit a cigarette and waited for the agonized man to continue. "My contact wouldn't carry me. I needed the stuff."

Roper asked the name of the contact, and it was a *paisano* already known to him.

"He offered me a proposition for a good price, and I took it. He got Blaney to hire me." The lining of his stomach felt as though it was being grated by barbed wire, and the policemen waited patiently for his groaning to abate. "Certain shipments of figurines contained H. Those invoices had a special code number. Blaney never knew what was going on. If he suspected, he never let on. The boys wouldn't trust anything like this to him. He's a shmuck. Only the fakes worried him."

He bit the pillow again and for a moment it seemed he was on the verge of shrieking. After a series of staccato gasps he resumed speaking.

"I got greedy. I began stealing some figurines. First I planned the way to keep the finger off me. Toni helped because I had her hooked . . . in all ways. I gave the figurines to Tippy after emptying them. He never knew they held H. I slipped him some of the genuines too. I had to make it look good."

"Tippy never stole any on his own." It was Max

speaking, though Roper didn't recognize the voice.

"No," whispered Cardew. "The only reason Blaney fingered the kid was to frighten him into spilling who was actually responsible for the thefts. I knew Tippy wouldn't betray me. We were good friends now. He saw a lot of me and Toni. He liked Toni. It might have meant trouble for her too. He protected us."

Max held the syringe like a dagger. He was frozen to the wall.

"But Sunday . . . he needed five hundred dollars."

Two minutes were spent waiting for an attack of the dry heaves to subside.

"Toni was with me at the apartment. We were high. The kid thought we were drunk. I didn't have any five hundred and I told him so. The monkeys were in the room. We were too gone to notice him pocket one. Later, after he left, I wanted another shot. The monkey with the H was missing. I thought Toni took it. But she didn't. It was the kid. I panicked. I had to find him before he knew what was in it."

His eyes caressed the syringe.

"I called Bibi. She said she thought he might be at home. I went looking for him. I went to Blaney's place and saw the kid coming out with his face bleeding. I trailed him to the loft. I cornered him. He was weak from the beating Blaney gave him. He wouldn't tell me where he hid the monkey. I got mad. I broke his neck."

(Max'll break that goddamn syringe, thought Roper.)

Cardew continued with an effort. "When Tippy was reported missing, Toni . . . my darling Antonia . . . got suspicious. She was so far gone on H, there was no controlling her. Yesterday she began getting desperate. I only had enough for myself. I told her I didn't have any, or any money to buy any . . . and the *paisanos* were on my neck about the stolen H . . . and I looked at my beautiful Antonia and knew here was my out. She was threatening to tell Blaney everything. I told her to hold out until today's shipment . . . and it came . . . and I went to meet her in the car. I set the appointment for shortly after five"—he clutched at his stomach—"when I knew there'd be no attendant, and I broke her neck." He stared at the syringe and licked his lips hungrily. "Killing two's just as easy as killing one. *Gimme the goddamn shot!*"

Max's fingers parted slowly and the syringe crashed to the floor and shattered. Max started to lunge at Cardew, but Roper intercepted and forced him back against the wall.

"Let me hit him!" cried Max. "Let me hit him!"

Cardew stared dumbly at the shattered syringe.

"Beautiful," he whispered. "Beautiful."

It was a simple eulogy, a blessedly simple one, and Max hoped it would also be blessedly brief. He had choked up twice in the past five minutes, and knew if he choked up a third time, he would lose control. (Me. The iceberg. The stoic. The disinterested. It takes a murdered teen-ager to make a dent in me. Not my own son. Somebody else's. Now I miss them both. Sylvia Plotkin understood, talking till three in the morning Thursday night in her tidy Plotkin apartment. Sylvia understood, and now that gives me a person with which to share. And she keeps herself at arm's length, which is good. She isn't pushing. She isn't misreading me. She knows how to handle.)

He was choking up again.

Sylvia tried to ignore Max's wheezing by concentrating on the young priest, who didn't seem to have the strength to talk above a whisper. (Why the secret, padre? The whole country has heard of Henry Thorpe Blaney. He's made headlines. Attention has been paid. *Sappho*'s publishing a retrospective of his poetry. The kid's made it big. *Speak up.*)

She wished the boy had been Jewish. Then there would have been passion, heartbreak, and borscht-red regret exploding all over the cemetery. (Give me a good old-fashioned orthodox rabbi with a flowing black beard and a rich silvery tenor. *They* know how to eulogize. *They* know how to shatter your heart, pierce your soul, dissolve you to tears. They *really* know how to make you feel a loss . . . Why isn't anybody *crying?*)

Wilma Blaney felt her left leg going to sleep. (Come on already. Get it over with. Lower the coffin and let's go. Ashes to ashes dust to dust my foot. Whatever became of an eye for an eye? That boat sails in three hours and I've still got some packing to do. Ah Rio! *Ri-o-o-o by the sea-o-o-o!*) Madame Vilna poked her. She hadn't realized she was humming.

Madame Vilna's black satin dress with the bugle beads had made its debut onstage at the Yiddish Art Theater on Second Avenue four decades ago, when she made a memorable entrance tied to the back of a black stallion in *Ich Hub Nisht Mairer* (*Mazeppa*). But the dress was still serviceable and Sylvia Plotkin had admired it. Vilna disapproved thoroughly of the young priest. She disapproved thoroughly of anyone who couldn't project. Tippeleh could project. With both hands she held the scrolls she had herself devised of two inside cylinders from toilet rolls, and with loving care had pasted to the cylinders the sheet of paper on which she had neatly lettered one of Tippy's poems. (Comes *my* turn, will they get *projection.*)

Basil Kirby stood rigidly, with his head bowed. (The insurance will cover the loss of the car. The piece-goods samples can be easily replaced. Even some of the cash the kid stole is covered by the insurance. Lois' apartment isn't really big enough for the two of us, but we can make do for the time being.) He cast a sideways glance at the grieving mother. (Good heavens, she's smiling.)

An echo chamber in Lois Corey's brain reverberated with the voice of an eight-year-old boy. (I love you, Aunt Lois. I love you better than anybody, but don't tell Mommy cause she'll be jealous.

Dear Aunt Lois I love you best,
I love you better than all the rest,
Now and forever, right to the end,
I promise to always be your friend.

Take another chocolate, darling.
I am calm. I am peaceful. I am serene.)

The sound waves of a shattering sob broke into Sylvia Plotkin's reverie. She looked across the coffin at the tear-stained face. (All right, Rodriguez. No deportation.)

The hospital room had bars on the windows. Marcus Blaney was propped up in bed, his head bandaged, his left leg with its plaster cast suspended in midair by a hoist. He wiped the palms of his hands on the bedcover and blinked his frog eyes nervously. (If I beat the rap like my lawyer says I just might possibly with any luck, I'll clear out. As far away from here as I can get. Away from the *paisanos* and Van Larsen and Lois and that stinking *putana* Wilma. I'll go someplace they'll never think of finding me. *Rio.*)

Clifton Southford sat in the Eames chair, sipping champagne, rubbing his bare feet together, and fingering the Delft oriole. He scowled at Tippy's "creation." The money. The money it took to squash the late unpleasantness. What a dreadful loss on a five-dollar investment! The promise the judge had extracted from Southford's fashionable lawyer that the sculptor would enter psychiatric treatment immediately. Genius is entitled to its pecul*iar*ities! He flung the figurine at the "creation." A shiver went up his spine.

The figurine hadn't broken.

Green Teeth stared with purple disbelief at the man in the white suit in the gray cubicle of the free clinic.

"The tests are positive," said the doctor, "you're venereal."

Sweat-drenched, Edmund Cardew lay huddled in a corner of the hospital bed in his cell, no longer struggling against the thick straps that tied him to the mattress. The hallucinations were passing. The one or two he remembered were brilliantly colorful. If they'd only let him have some paints and canvas. He'd show them greatness. He'd show that Van Larsen. He was laying out the canvas in his mind. A boy's head and a woman's head, both hanging grotesquely from broken necks. Across the two heads, the outline of a syringe.

Beautiful! Beautiful!

Bibi Dumas stared out of the window of the Greyhound Bus at the passing countryside. Her purse rested on her lap. In it were newspaper clippings. She had thoroughly worked out the story for her and the family to tell nosy, gossiping neighbors. My husband was murdered. Here. You can read it yourself. The *Post* even promises its readers a page of his poetry in the weekend edition. It's being sent to me. Bless Satan. I'll miss him.

(Should I have told Tippy the truth, she asked herself for the umpteenth time. Would he be alive today if I had told him the truth? Why did I feel it so necessary to preserve his romantic illusions about me. I didn't love him. He was a nice kid and kind of sexy for seventeen. I really think I would have told him the truth the day I phoned his house to tell him I'm going back to Chicago. I really think I would have.

Hell.

How could I have told him the baby's father is that hophead artist?)

Sylvia Plotkin had just finished doing her nails when the phone rang. Hearing his voice on the other end, she hugged the phone tightly.

"I know it's a little sudden, said Max Van Larsen, "but it looks like I'm free tonight, after all. Would you like to have dinner?"

"I'd *love* to," gurgled Sylvia Plotkin, "except I have a suggestion." (Be still, my heart.) "Instead of going to some noisy restaurant and eating a greasy meal and watching you pop tablets in your mouth" (such a Kirk Douglas mouth) "why don't you come up here for some genuine home cooking? If I have to say so myself" (God helps those who help themselves) "I'm a pretty good cook. That's *one* thing my Isaac" (if *you* ever got a look at Max Van Larsen) "never complained about."

"You really feel like cooking?" asked Max, his fingers trailing across the gift-wrapped package that contained an LP of the late Edith Sitwell reading her own poetry, purchased on impulse for Sylvia Plotkin.

"Why else would I suggest it? I could make a simple pot roast" (an extremely fine cut of meat) "with browned potatoes" (in pure creamery butter) "and a salad" (no cucumbers or green peppers to aggravate your ulcer) "and at this *very* moment on the stove, I'm simmering a pot of my *very own* chicken soup!" She crossed two fingers. "You *love* chicken soup, don't you?"

"The menu sounds great," said Max. "Eight o'clock okay?"

"Eight o'clock perfect. See you then."

Sylvia killed two birds with one stone. She waved her fingers in the air from the sheer joy of the prospect of watching Max Van Larsen spooning her chicken soup, and maybe the damn fingernails would dry quicker.

Chicken soup. Max smiled, shook his head and rummaged in the top drawer of his desk for the bottle of tablets.

I loathe chicken soup.

GEORGE BAXT
His Life and Hard Times

On a Monday afternoon, June 11, 1923, George Baxt was born on a kitchen table in Brooklyn.

He was nine when his first published work appeared in the Brooklyn *Times-Union.* He received between two and five dollars for each little story or poem the paper used.

His first play was produced when he was eighteen. It lasted one night.

Mr. Baxt has been a propagandist for Voice of America, a press agent, and an actors' agent. He has written extensively for stage, screen, and television. During stays in England in the fifties and sixties, he wrote a number of films *(Circus of Horrors, Horror Hotel, Burn Witch, Burn)* which are now staples of late night television.

His first novel, A QUEER KIND OF DEATH, was published in 1966. His other novels include SWING LOW, SWEET HARRIET; A PARADE OF COCKEYED CREATURES; TOPSY AND EVIL; "I!" SAID THE DEMON; PROCESS OF ELIMINATION; THE DOROTHY PARKER MURDER CASE; and most recently THE ALFRED HITCHCOCK MURDER CASE.

Mr. Baxt lives in New York, is a bachelor, and is devoted to his VCR.

THE LIBRARY OF CRIME CLASSICS®

George Baxt
THE DOROTHY PARKER MURDER CASE
0-930330-36-6 288pp $4.95

A QUEER KIND OF DEATH
0-930330-46-3 250pp $4.95

A PARADE OF COCKEYED CREATURES
0-930330-47-1 250pp $4.95

Anthony Boucher
NINE TIMES NINE
0-930330-37-4 256pp $4.95

Caryl Brahms & S.J. Simon
A BULLET IN THE BALLET
0-930330-12-9 159pp $4.95

MURDER A LA STROGANOFF
0-930330-33-1 274pp $4.95

SIX CURTAINS FOR STROGANOVA
0-930330-49-8 250pp $4.95

Christianna Brand
CAT AND MOUSE
0-930330-18-8 200pp $4.95

John Dickson Carr

BELOW SUSPICION
0-930330-50-1 186pp $4.95

THE BURNING COURT
0-930330-27-7 215pp $4.95

DEATH TURNS THE TABLES
0-930330-22-6 200pp $4.95

HAG'S NOOK
0-930330-28-5 192pp $4.95

HE WHO WHISPERS
0-930330-38-2 176pp $4.95

THE PROBLEM OF THE
GREEN CAPSULE
0-930330-51-X 223pp $4.95

THE SLEEPING SPHINX
0-930330-24-2 199pp $4.95

THE THREE COFFINS
0-930330-39-0 256pp $4.95

TILL DEATH DO US PART
0-930330-21-8 200pp $4.95

Carroll John Daly

MURDER FROM THE EAST
0-930330-01-3 312pp $4.95

Lillian De La Torre

DR. SAM: JOHNSON, DETECTOR
0-930330-08-0 261pp $4.95

THE DETECTIONS OF
DR. SAM: JOHNSON
0-930330-09-9 190pp $4.95

THE RETURN OF DR. SAM:
JOHNSON, DETECTOR
0-930330-34-X 200pp $4.95

Dashiell Hammett
& Alex Raymond
SECRET AGENT X-9
0-930330-05-6 225pp $9.95

James Gollin
ELIZA'S GALIARDO
0-930330-54-4 180pp $4.95

THE PHILOMEL FOUNDATION
0-930330-40-4 208pp $4.95

Richard Hull
THE MURDER OF MY AUNT
0-930330-02-1 174pp $4.95

Victoria Lincoln
A PRIVATE DISGRACE
LIZZIE BORDEN BY DAYLIGHT
0-930330-35-8 320pp $5.95

Barry N. Malzberg
UNDERLAY
0-930330-41-2 256pp $4.95

Margaret Millar
AN AIR THAT KILLS
0-930330-23-4 247pp $4.95

ASK FOR ME TOMORROW
0-930330-15-3 179pp $4.95

BANSHEE
0-930330-14-5 202pp $4.95

BEAST IN VIEW
0-930330-07-2 251pp $4.95

BEYOND THIS POINT
ARE MONSTERS
0-930330-31-5 213pp $4.95

THE CANNIBAL HEART
0-930330-32-3 207pp $4.95

THE FIEND
0-930330-10-2 245pp $4.95

HOW LIKE AN ANGEL
0-930330-04-8 279pp $4.95

THE LISTENING WALLS
0-930330-52-8 250pp $4.95

A STRANGER IN MY GRAVE
0-930330-06-4 311pp $4.95

ROSE'S LAST SUMMER
0-930330-26-9 223pp $4.95

WALL OF EYES
0-930330-42-0 224pp $4.95

William F. Nolan
SPACE FOR HIRE
0-930330-19-6 200pp $4.95

LOOK OUT FOR SPACE
0-930330-20-X 192pp $4.95

Ellery Queen
THE TRAGEDY OF X
0-930330-43-9 256pp $4.95

THE TRAGEDY OF Y
0-930330-53-6 244pp $4.95

Clayton Rawson
DEATH FROM A TOP HAT
0-930330-44-7 288pp $4.95